FINAL VENDETTA

USA TODAY BESTSELLING AUTHOR

T.K. LEIGH

FINAL VENDETTA

Published by Carpe Per Diem Publishing, Inc

Cover Design: Cat Head Media, Inc.

Cover assets:

Used under license from Deposit Photos and Adobe Stock © 2025

BOOKS BY T.K. LEIGH

ROMANTIC SUSPENSE

The Saint Trilogy

Cruel Saint

Tempting Devil

Final Vendetta

The Temptation Series

Temptation

Persuasion

Provocation

Obsession

The Broken Crown Trilogy

Royal Creed

Fallen Knight

Broken Crown

The Inferno Saga
Part One: Spark
Part Two: Smoke
Part Three: Flame
Part Four: Burn

The Possession Duet
Possession
Atonement

The Beautiful Mess Series
A Beautiful Mess
A Tragic Wreck
Gorgeous Chaos

The Deception Duet
Chasing the Dragon
Slaying the Dragon

Beautiful Mess World Standalones
Heart of Light
Heart of Marley
Vanished

For a free eBook, sign up for T.K.'s newsletter.

Some of T.K. Leigh's books may contain content that could be triggering for sensitive readers. For a full list of content warnings for each book and/or series, please visit her website by scanning the code below.

CHAPTER ONE

Gideon

The city lights zoomed past the window as we careened down the freeway, Henry's hands gripping the wheel so hard his knuckles were white.

I struggled to process what led to this moment, my mind a blur. All I could see was the image that had flashed across the television screen mere minutes ago.

James Turner's car speeding recklessly through the streets of Santa Monica.

The crunching impact as he slammed into another SUV.

The twisted metal wreckage that had become of the car.

Henry's hesitant voice telling me the car he hit belonged to Imogene.

"Breathe, Gideon." Henry broke through my thoughts, his eyes sharp with worry as he glanced my way. "It'll be okay."

"Okay?" I scoffed bitterly.

My voice didn't sound like my own. It sounded far away. Like all of this was a horrible dream.

How I wished that were true.

"Imogene is hurt because of me, Henry. I don't even know if…"

I couldn't bring myself to say it out loud, my biggest fear clawing its way through me from the inside out.

For the first time since this nightmare began, my carefully constructed façade had begun to crumble. I'd spent years learning how to keep every emotion and impulse buried beneath a mask that never slipped. But tonight? My chest felt like it was caving in.

I'd been so damn focused on settling the score, blinded by the need to make those who'd taken everything from me pay. But in my obsession, I hadn't seen the potential price someone else might pay.

I hadn't seen the price *Imogene* might pay.

She'd left me because of this, walked away from the darkness I'd let consume me. I convinced myself it was for the best. That I was on a suicide mission anyway.

Now, there was a very real possibility Imogene could be dead.

Because of me.

The thought made me sick.

I gripped the seat tightly as dread gnawed at my insides. This wasn't how it was supposed to end. This wasn't what I wanted when I started down this road.

"We don't know anything yet," Henry tried to assure me in the calm, collected way he did everything. "Just stay positive."

I pressed my hands into fists, resisting the urge to slam them into the dashboard as Henry raced down another stretch of road. Everything about this night felt like a punishment, like karma coming back to collect what was due. Each second brought a fresh wave of panic, outrage, and guilt crashing over me. I was unraveling, the pieces of who I was scattered like debris on the side of that road with the remnants of Imogene's shattered car.

When we screeched to a stop in front of the hospital's emergency entrance, I flung open the door and sprinted toward an ambulance that had just arrived, red and blue lights casting harsh shadows across the pavement.

My heart thrashed in my chest as I watched the hospital staff rush toward the ambulance, hurriedly pulling out a stretcher.

And lying on that stretcher, Imogene's broken body was barely recognizable.

An oxygen mask covered her nose and mouth, blood

streaked across her face and arms. Any control I'd managed to retain over the past few minutes crumbled, leaving only raw terror.

My feet moved of their own accord, driven by the desperate need to feel her skin against mine. To feel some sort of reassurance she wouldn't die because of my actions. But as I approached, a member of the hospital staff stepped in front of me, her expression firm.

"Sir, please stay back."

But I couldn't stay back. Not when it came to Imogene.

"You don't understand. I need to know if she's going to be okay. She's—"

My voice cracked under the weight of helplessness consuming me. I hadn't felt anything remotely close to this since I woke up in a cold cell and learned my fate.

"Please," I begged, hoping this woman who'd probably witnessed death on a daily basis would show me compassion.

"We'll do everything we can for her," she assured me, but her words felt empty. She probably said the same thing to everyone in my shoes. "But to do that, I need you to stay back."

I wanted to shake her, force her to tell me what I needed to hear. But I stayed rooted in place, watching them wheel Imogene inside, my only tether to this world slipping farther away with each step.

I thought I'd faced hell in all its forms. Survived horrors beyond imagination and lost parts of myself I knew I would never get back.

That was nothing compared to this.

A hand landed on my shoulder, and I whirled around, staring into Henry's green eyes.

"Let them work, Gideon. She's in the best hands now."

His words were supposed to reassure me, but they didn't. They couldn't. Because none of this should have happened. The one person I'd tried to keep safe, the one person I'd wanted to protect from everything I'd become, was now lying on an operating table, her life hanging by a thread.

All because of me.

Confucius warned when starting out on a journey of revenge to dig two graves.

I didn't anticipate that one of those graves would belong to Imogene.

CHAPTER TWO

Gideon

The clock on the wall ticked, each second dragging me closer to the edge of sanity as I paced the length of the waiting room, counting every tile, every chair. Anything to keep me from giving in to the help-lessness taking root in my chest.

Minutes felt like hours. Every second that passed without an update only twisted the knife deeper. Henry watched me with cautious scrutiny, but he knew better than to say anything. This was one fight he couldn't help me win.

As I paced, I tried to shake the image of Imogene's crumpled car or the blood staining her blonde hair, the bruises already darkening her skin. My mind reeled back to the sight of her on that stretcher — how still she had been.

Too still.

She'd walked away from me once, furious at the man I'd become, and I couldn't bear the thought that she might leave for good this time.

There was nothing I could do to bring her back.

The worst part about all of this had been calling Imogene's mom to tell her what had happened. To hear the worry and panic in her voice.

And it was all my fault.

The sharp crackle of the TV sliced through the quiet room, and I darted my gaze toward it as the eleven o'clock news began its broadcast. The top news story was about the police pursuit from earlier. The newscaster droned on, his voice hollow, detached.

"Earlier tonight, Senator James Turner led police in a high-speed chase through Santa Monica following the release of a recording implicating him in the coverup of a murder five years ago. He's currently in critical condition after crashing his vehicle. For more details, let's go to Lexi Rhymes at the scene of the crash."

My blood boiled as I listened to this reporter talk about James Turner and what his current condition might mean for his senate seat without a single mention of the woman he hit.

"Turn it off," I barked at the receptionist, my voice tight with barely contained fury. "Turn it off right now. She's fighting for her life in there because of that man."

The receptionist's eyes widened in shock before she quickly grabbed the remote and changed the channel to some mindless home renovation show. But it didn't matter. The damage was done. The image of Turner's mangled car served as a reminder of the role I played in all of this.

"Gideon," Henry cautioned in a low, steady voice — the tone of someone trying to keep a bomb from going off. "Losing it won't help her."

"I'm not 'losing it,'" I snapped back, though we both knew that was a lie. I was hanging on by a thread.

Jumping to my feet, I crossed the waiting room toward the reception desk, forcing myself to keep my voice even.

"I need an update on Imogene Prescott's condition. I've been waiting for hours."

The receptionist gave me a pitying look before telling me the same line I'd heard a dozen times since arriving. "I'm sorry, sir. As I've already told you, only immediate family can be updated on her condition."

I clenched my jaw, fighting the urge to argue. "What's it going to take to get some information? A donation to the hospital? Do you need a new cancer wing or something? Consider it done. Just..." I swallowed down the painful lump in my throat. "Don't let her die."

"I truly am sorry, sir. When her parents arrive, they can sign the forms allowing us to speak to you. Until then, I can't tell you anything."

I squeezed my eyes shut, pushing down my frustration.

I was teetering on the edge of sanity, rage simmering beneath my skin, threatening to boil over. I wanted to scream, to break something, to do anything to dispel the hopelessness that clung to me like a second skin.

I didn't know how much longer I could go without knowing if Imogene was still alive.

The sound of the automatic doors to the emergency room cut through, and I snapped my head toward them, praying it was Imogene's parents, even though the flight from Atlanta would take longer than the two hours it had been since I called them.

Instead of her parents, Melanie stood there, her face pale but resolute. She closed the distance between us quickly, her eyes searching mine as if it were the first time she was seeing me. In that moment, there was no doubt in my mind. She knew. Imogene told her the truth about who I really was.

When she threw her arms around me, I froze for a beat before returning her hug and pulling her close.

"Sam," she whispered, her voice inaudible to anyone but me.

"Yeah," I sighed, grateful to be myself around her again, even if I still wasn't sure who that was.

She pulled back and met my gaze, seeing the truth within. The rest of my features may have been completely different, but my eyes never changed. It was my eyes that gave me away to Imogene, despite her brain telling her it couldn't be.

"You really suck, you know that?" she choked out, playfully punching my arm before hugging me again. "But I'm so glad you're okay."

"It's my fault, Melanie," I admitted, my voice strained. "She's in there because of me." I glanced at the locked doors leading into the emergency wing.

"Were you driving the car that slammed into her?" She gave me a pointed glare.

"I'm the reason he fled from the police. If I hadn't—"

"No. Don't do that. This isn't your fault."

"I just... I hate feeling like this. I can't even get any information about her because I'm not technically family, regardless of how much money I promise to throw at this damn hospital." I shot a glare at the receptionist, even though she was just following protocol.

It still didn't make it sting any less.

"She'll pull through," Melanie assured me, placing

her hand on my arm and giving it a gentle squeeze. "Imogene is stronger than anyone I know."

I nodded, but I wasn't sure I believed her.

A man like me didn't deserve miracles.

And now Imogene would pay the price for my sins.

CHAPTER THREE

Gideon

Hours passed, each one more painful than the last. The waiting room grew quieter as night bled into early morning, leaving just the faint hum of fluorescent lights and the low murmur of hushed voices from the nurses' station. I'd lost track of how many times I'd counted the tiles on the ceiling, anything to distract myself from the overwhelming guilt crushing my chest.

Melanie rested her head on my shoulder, her arm looped through mine. I appreciated her presence right now, even if my nerves were frayed beyond repair. I needed this connection to someone close to Imogene.

"You'll get answers soon," she assured me in a soothing voice, sensing my unease.

Not like it was difficult. I'd never been so tense. So ready to snap.

"Her parents' plane landed a while ago so they should be here any minute."

As if on cue, the emergency room doors slid open. Julia and Lachlan rushed into the waiting room, looking strained and worried, but determined. We all shot to our feet, and I felt a jolt in my chest when Julia's gaze fell on Henry, her brow furrowing in confusion.

After all, she knew Henry from when I was Samuel Tate. Not as Gideon Saint.

She blinked several times, probably trying to make sense of this tangled web I had spun around myself.

When she looked back at me, she swept her analytical gaze over my features, as if mentally rearranging my face, readjusting the shape of my jaw and straightening my nose. Then she pushed out a shuttering sigh.

Without a second's hesitation, she moved across the room and wrapped her arms around me in a fierce, motherly embrace.

"Imogene was right," she whispered. "She mentioned she thought it might be you."

I nodded, guilt crashing over me like a wave. "I'm sorry, Ms. Hale," I murmured, my voice rough. I didn't embellish further. I couldn't. There was so much for me to be sorry for.

For thinking I could use Imogene as bait.

For lying to her.

For being the reason she was currently in the hospital, fighting for her life.

If she was still alive at all.

"You have nothing to be sorry for." She pulled back, searching my expression. "You're alive. She always questioned if you were. Said if you were really dead, she'd feel it." Julia laughed under her breath. "I convinced her she needed to move on for her own good. That she'd drive herself crazy if she kept living in the past. I'm happy I was wrong. So happy," she murmured as she wrapped me in another tight hug before stepping back and composing herself. "I'll get some answers."

"Thank you," I said around a rush of relief.

"Of course." She held my gaze for a beat, then moved toward Lachlan, who studied me with a mixture of confusion and skepticism. But it only lasted a second before Julia pulled him toward the nurses' station.

I kept my focus glued on them, trying to eavesdrop on their conversation to find out anything I possibly could about Imogene's condition. But instead of telling them anything, the nurse stated that the doctor overseeing Imogene's treatment had asked to speak with them, then led them through the secured door. But before they disappeared, Julia passed me a reassuring smile.

It did nothing to help, though.

I couldn't help but fear the worst. That the doctor had asked to speak with them privately so he could deliver the bad news away from prying eyes and ears.

I tried to take a deep breath to calm myself. Remind myself to think positive. But it was impossible. The waiting room felt smaller now.

Too small.

Every moment spent here only reminded me of how powerless I was. I couldn't sit here any longer, suffocating under the weight of it all.

"I need some air," I barked out at Melanie and Henry, though I doubted fresh air would help.

Then I spun on my heels and headed toward the sliding doors. But before I stepped outside, I noticed a sign for the chapel. I'd never been one to pray, especially these past few years.

Right now, I was willing to try anything.

I followed the quiet hallway until I reached a pair of large wooden doors that seemed out of place in such a sterile and brightly lit environment. Pushing one open, I entered the darkened space, its dim light a stark contrast to the harsh fluorescent outside. A stained-glass feature made up the far wall behind the altar, a long table in the back of the room covered with candles in red votives, some flickering with life while others remained unlit.

Sinking into a pew, I bowed my head and closed my eyes. It had been years since I'd been in a place like this.

Since I'd spoken to anyone who might be listening on the other side.

I didn't know if God could hear me, or if He would even care. Hell, I wasn't even sure He existed anymore.

I'd spent so many years consumed by vengeance, certain nothing in this world — or the next — could save me. But this wasn't for me. This was for Imogene.

"If she pulls through," I murmured, barely able to hear my own words. "I'll walk away from all of it. I'll... I'll find a way to turn over a new leaf. I won't let revenge ruin anything else. I'll only focus on her. On my future. Not be so obsessed with my past. Please..." I looked up at the ceiling. "Please don't make her pay for what I've done."

The heavy wooden door creaked open, causing an echo to reverberate through the silent room. I snapped my head toward the sound as Lachlan slipped inside. Approaching me, he arched a single eyebrow, silently asking permission to join me.

I nodded, and he lowered himself beside me, keeping his gaze focused straight ahead for several long moments. I wanted to ask what the doctor told him.

At the same time, I didn't.

I wanted to remain in this moment when I still had hope, regardless of how fleeting it was. Wanted to stay in a world where Imogene was still in it.

"Julia told me who you really are," Lachlan finally

said in a subtle Australian accent, his tone more matter-of-fact than accusatory. "That your name isn't actually Gideon Saint."

"It's not," I confirmed.

"Does Imogene know? Julia mentioned she was suspicious, but—"

"She does now. She didn't at first, but I eventually told her the truth."

He nodded, processing my confession for what felt like an eternity. Then his eyes met mine, steady and searching.

"I don't know what happened to you, why the world thought you were dead. And maybe I don't want to know. But Imogene...she deserves someone who will put her first. Above everything else." He gave me a knowing look. "Do you understand that?"

The question hung between us, heavy with implication. I tried not to read too much into his use of the present tense when speaking of Imogene, although it certainly gave me hope. If he'd received the news I feared most, he wouldn't make me promise to put her first. Would he?

"Without a doubt. She's... She's everything to me."

Satisfied with my assurance, Lachlan placed a hand on my shoulder. "Good." He gave it a brief squeeze before releasing me, looking forward once more. Another heavy silence filled the room before he announced, "She's out of surgery."

A sudden, almost unbearable relief washed over me. Every muscle in my body relaxed, and I closed my eyes, silently thanking God, Allah, the universe for listening to my desperate pleas.

"She has some cracked ribs," he continued, "but they'll heal on their own in time. They had to remove her spleen and re-inflate a collapsed lung, and they'll have to keep the chest tube in over the next three or so days to help. Her shoulder was dislocated, but they set it during surgery. In addition to a concussion, she has a lot of other bruising and the doctor expects her to be in quite a bit of pain when she wakes up, which is why he wants to keep her sedated for the time being. But she's expected to make a full recovery with plenty of rest."

"And her heart?" I asked.

"It's strong."

I exhaled, the tightness in my chest finally releasing with my breath. She was going to be okay. I hadn't lost her.

And I was going to do everything in my power not to squander this second chance.

CHAPTER FOUR

Gideon

My footsteps echoed in the quiet hospital corridor as Lachlan led me toward Imogene's recovery room. My heart pounded with anxiety as we navigated the maze of hallways, the fluorescent lights overhead casting an unnatural glow. The air was heavy with the sharp scent of disinfectant and the faint undertone of sickness — a reminder of the fragility of life.

Despite Lachlan's assurances that Imogene was stable and would make a full recovery, I wouldn't believe it until I saw her with my own eyes. Until I heard her heart beat. Until I felt the warmth of her skin.

Finally, we reached the end of the corridor and Lachlan opened the door for me. On a hard swallow, I entered the room, my gaze immediately drawn to

Imogene lying in the bed. Melanie and Julia sat in chairs beside her, their faces filled with relief. But all I could see was Imogene, bruised and broken from my actions.

I took a shaky step closer, my heart constricting at the sight of the tubes and wires snaking from her body, just as Lachlan had warned me. Her left arm was wrapped in a sling, a bandage covered her eyebrow, and bruises decorated her skin. I could only imagine the bruises I couldn't see.

It took everything in me not to collapse right there, my knees shaking as I fought to keep steady. A choked sob escaped before I could stop it, and Julia rushed toward me, placing a comforting hand on my arm.

"She's alive. She's fine."

I nodded numbly, unable to find the words. The weight of my actions bore down on me with a crushing force. I did this to her. Imogene was here because of me. Because of my obsession with revenge.

I'd never forgive myself for this.

"We're going to the hotel now that she's stable," Julia said after a beat. "The doctors have assured us she'll be in good hands. I also gave them permission to discuss her treatment with you until she wakes up in case any decisions need to be made." She looked at me, her eyes warm and kind. "But you should get some rest, too."

"I'll rest when she's awake," I ground out, my eyes burning with unshed tears.

"It might be a while."

"I'm not leaving her. Never again."

With an understanding smile, she nodded. Lachlan placed a hand on my shoulder as he passed in silent reassurance before following Julia into the hallway.

"You'll keep me posted?" Melanie asked, and I shifted my gaze toward her as she approached.

"Of course."

"Thanks," she responded around a yawn.

"How are you getting home?"

"My car."

I shook my head and reached inside my suit jacket for my phone. "Henry will take you."

"I'll be fine. I—"

When I narrowed my stare on her, she snapped her mouth shut, obviously aware it was a lost cause. After what happened to Imogene, I didn't want to risk Melanie getting behind the wheel in her exhausted state.

"Thank you," she said as she wrapped her arms around me.

I pulled her close, leaving a soft kiss on her head. "Be safe."

"Always."

Then she turned from me and disappeared down the hallway, the door clicking shut behind her.

Pushing out a long sigh, I returned my attention to Imogene, erasing the distance between me and her bed.

As I lowered myself into the chair, I gently took her hand in mine, worried the slightest pressure might break her. Her skin was cool and smooth beneath my thumb, fragile in a way I'd never known her to be. She'd always been strong, resilient, never bending no matter how much the world tried to crush her.

But now?

Now she was here, bruised and battered, her breaths shallow but steady, reminding me what I'd almost lost.

Reminding me of the role I played in putting her here.

"I'm so sorry, Imogene." My voice cracked with emotion as I pressed a tender kiss to her hand. "I should have known something like this could happen. I just never..." I trailed off, a hollow ache settling in my chest.

I'd spent the past year obsessed with revenge, trying to find closure in destruction. And for what? To risk Imogene's life? Was it really worth it? Had it *ever* been worth it?

"No more," I declared with nothing short of determination.

I let my statement hang in the silence, the words a pledge. A commitment binding me to something bigger than revenge. Bigger than my anger. Bigger than my hatred.

I'd give Imogene the future she deserved, even if it

meant walking away from the only thing that kept me alive in that hellish prison.

But now that I thought about it, I knew the truth. It wasn't just revenge that kept me going. It was Imogene. I planned to do everything in my power to prove to her I was no longer that person.

"No more lies. No more revenge." I swallowed hard. "No more Gideon Saint."

CHAPTER FIVE

Gideon

The hallway outside Imogene's room was a little brighter than the night before, yet the guilt hadn't lessened. I'd barely slept, but it didn't matter. Imogene was stable, recovering. That was the only important thing right now.

When I walked into the waiting area, Henry was still there, sitting in a chair with his legs stretched out in front of him and arms folded, his eyes closed. Despite all the times I told him he didn't need to stay, he refused to leave, staying not just for Imogene, but also for me.

He truly was a good friend.

When I finally escaped the hell I'd been trapped in, he was the first person who came to mind. He was the one person I knew who would believe me. Who would help.

And over the past year, that was precisely what he did.

He may have occasionally questioned whether this was the right path, but I knew it came from a place of love. After all, if anyone would understand my need to even the score, it was Henry Fontaine.

But that was over now.

As I approached him, he blinked his eyes open and straightened.

"I didn't mean to wake you," I told him.

He waved off my apology. "How's she doing?"

I lowered myself into the chair beside him. "Still sleeping." I wished I had more news, but there hadn't been any changes over the past several hours.

I shifted my gaze toward the windows that over-looked the busy sidewalks three stories below. Reporters swarmed like vultures, each one hoping to catch a sound bite about the high-speed chase that resulted in a woman nearly losing her life. They didn't care about the actual human cost. They just wanted a sensational story to sell.

"Any news on Turner?" I asked, shifting my gaze toward Henry. I'd purposefully avoided the news all day, going so far as turning off my phone.

Anyone who needed to get in touch with me knew where I was.

He leaned closer. "The doctors don't expect him to wake up. Apparently, he's officially brain dead. He's being kept alive by machines for the time being until his wife can get here and make a decision."

"I see." I nodded as I processed this news.

After the role James Turner played in what happened to me as well as Jonah Pruitt, I should have been thrilled by the news that he was essentially a vegetable. It was the same situation Jonah had been in after James paid several inmates to silence him. James Turner would never leave this hospital alive. It was exactly what I wanted for him.

But any sense of vindication or poetic justice came with a sour taste in my mouth. The satisfaction I once thought would come with his demise was hollow. Especially now that I realized the true price of my revenge.

"And Liam?" I asked after a beat, trying to keep my voice even.

Henry blew out a long breath, running a hand over his face. "No one knows where he is. Which doesn't look good, considering he already had heat on him from the body unexpectedly found on his boat." He gave me a knowing look.

"Couple that with the fact that he's been withdrawing large amounts of cash from his accounts since Brian McGuire's disappearance, it looks like he's on the run." He lowered his voice. "Do you want me to see what I can find?"

I pinched my lips together, hesitating. As if some part of me still resisted the changed course I set upon last night.

But I made a promise to God. Or maybe a deal with the devil. I wasn't sure which. All I did know was I wouldn't do anything to put Imogene's life in jeopardy again.

"It's over," I announced firmly, trying to push away any lingering doubts or reservations.

Henry scrunched his brow. "What do you mean?"

"All of it," I replied under my breath. "I'm done. No more revenge. No more lies. It's over. I appreciate everything you've done to help me, no questions asked..."

"You're my brother, even if not by blood. You'd do the same for me."

"Without a doubt. But I can't keep going down this path now that I finally know the cost." I glanced down the hallway in the direction of Imogene's room.

"I don't know what she'll want when she wakes up, but I'm going to spend the rest of my life trying to prove myself worthy of her. I have a second chance with the woman of my dreams. At least I *hope* I do. I'm not going to let anything stand in my way."

Henry narrowed his gaze. "If you're certain."

"I am." I held his gaze for a beat. "Just do me one last favor before you head back to your fortress of solitude."

He laughed slightly at my reference to his imposing home on the outskirts of Atlanta. "What's that?"

"Find me a house. A small place by the beach for Imogene. Something quiet, a little shack even. Somewhere she can breathe again. Where we can both breathe again. Somewhere untainted by all of this." I waved my hand around.

"Consider it done."

With a squeeze of my arm, he stood and disappeared from view, his phone already pressed to his ear.

I slunk back into my chair, my mind consumed with thoughts of James and Liam. Was I being foolish by not going after him? Or, at the very least, by not asking Henry to use his resources and expertise to locate him?

I had to remind myself I was done with that part of my life. I knew the cost now.

No more.

No matter how tempting it was to fall back on my old habits.

A movement caught my attention, and I snapped my head up to see Julia and Lachlan emerge from the hallway.

I jumped to my feet, my eyes brimming with hope. "Is she awake?"

"Not yet," Lachlan replied evenly.

"It's just a waiting game at this point," Julia added. "Nothing else we can do."

I nodded, hating this feeling of helplessness. I knew Imogene was okay and that the doctors were keeping her relatively sedated because of her pain, but I just wanted her to wake up.

"We're going to grab some lunch," Lachlan stated. "Would you like to come with us?"

I shook my head. "Thank you, but I'd rather stay here with her."

"Of course." Julia squeezed my hand. "We'll be back soon. You'll call if she wakes up?"

"Absolutely."

Once they left, I headed down the hallway and slipped inside Imogene's room, taking a seat beside her bed.

My gaze traveled over her still form, taking in every bruise, every bandage. The monitors beeped softly, a steady rhythm that reassured me with each beat.

Reaching for her hand, I gently traced my thumb over her knuckles, finding comfort in the feel of her skin as I thought back to everything we'd been through.

"Do you remember that trip to Hilton Head when we took Ollie to the beach?" I paused, letting the memory take shape, softening the ache in my chest.

"You'd convinced me to go running along the shore with you. Ollie thought it was the greatest game ever, him chasing us, us chasing each other. He got so worked up that he was tearing back and forth like a maniac."

A faint smile tugged at my lips, a tightness squeezing my chest. "After about an hour, we finally wore him out enough to sit down. It was perfect. Just us on the beach, watching as the sky turned every shade of pink and orange as we talked about all the places we wanted to go one day."

I tightened my grasp on her hand, my voice softer now. "I remember thinking that if I could freeze time and keep us in that moment forever, I'd do it. No worries. No secrets. Just you and me."

A small laugh escaped, quiet and bittersweet. "Then Ollie charged at us out of nowhere, barking his head off and dragging me back into the waves. You said—"

"Maybe next time you want to get laid on the beach, leave the dog at home."

Her words were no louder than a whisper, but they shot through me like a live wire. Less than twenty-four hours ago, I feared I'd never hear that sweet melody again.

I looked up sharply and met Imogene's eyes — hazy and barely open, but alive.

"You're awake," I said, my voice breaking with

emotion. Relief flooded through me, filling every crack, every scar.

She smiled weakly, her grip tightening around mine. "You're here."

"Always, Imogene." I brought her hand to my lips. "Always."

CHAPTER SIX

Imogene

My vision was blurry as I attempted to focus on my surroundings. The steady beeping, coupled with the strong scent of astringent, made it obvious I was in a hospital. But how did I get here?

I tried to put the pieces of last night together. At least I *hoped* it was only last night.

I recalled driving up to Santa Monica for a much-needed weekend with Melanie and telling her that Gideon was really Samuel. I'd even shared all the things he'd done, as well as all the things he still planned to do.

Instead of reassuring me I'd done the right thing by walking away, she convinced me his actions didn't make him a bad person. After all, my mother hadn't killed my father in self defense. She did so because she couldn't stomach the idea of living in a world with him in it anymore. Because if she didn't take his life, he would hurt more people.

The same could be said for Gideon.

I'd jumped into my car and sped toward the freeway, wanting to get home as quick as possible.

Wanting to get to *Gideon* as quick as possible.

The last thing I remembered was the sound of screeching tires and the scent of rubber.

Everything after that was a blur…

Until a few moments ago when a voice cut through the fog, talking about one of my favorite memories of Samuel at Hilton Head.

"How… How are you feeling?" Gideon asked, his worried gaze raking over my frame. I didn't even want to know how I looked right now. Not if how I felt was any indication.

"Like I've just been hit by a truck."

His expression fell and he pinched his eyes shut. "It's not that far from the truth."

"Hey." I squeezed his hand to the best of my ability. "I'm okay. At least I think I am."

He took a shuttering breath. "You are. You have a concussion, along with some broken ribs. Your lung collapsed, which is why there's a tube on your side. The doctors will most likely be able to remove it in the next day or two." His words came out even with a subtle tremble.

"You also no longer have a spleen. According to the doctor, it doesn't do much anyway, but you will be more susceptible to getting sick. Your shoulder was also dislocated, but they popped it back in during surgery."

"That explains the sling," I attempted to joke.

"I'll go tell the nurse you're awake so she can come talk to you. Or send the doctor in." He started to get up, but I stopped him.

"Not yet. I just want you to sit with me for a minute."

He lowered himself back into the chair, a small smile tugging on his lips. "Whatever you need." He brought my hand up to his mouth and touched a warm kiss to my skin.

"I was on my way to see you," I confessed after a moment of heavy silence, broken only by the steady beeping.

"What's that?"

"The night I was hit. I..." I scrunched my brows. "What day is it?"

"Sunday. You've only been out for a little over twelve hours."

"Good," I exhaled, somewhat relieved I hadn't lost too much time.

"But what do you mean you were on your way to see

me?" Concern and guilt flickered in his sparkling blue eyes.

"I told Mel everything, and she talked some sense into me. She reminded me there's a little darkness in all of us. I already lost you once. I didn't want to lose you again."

He stared at me, blinking repeatedly, before he jumped to his feet.

His reaction confused me. I thought he'd be relieved. But based on the way he paced the length of the hospital room, he looked more distraught than anything.

Despite the fact it was a Sunday afternoon, he wore a wrinkled tuxedo shirt and pants, as if he'd come here straight from some black-tie function. His bloodshot eyes suggested he hadn't slept a wink since arriving here.

"I didn't mean to upset you," I began tentatively, watching as he ran his hands through his disheveled hair. "I just finally realized that I overreacted when I heard you talking to Henry about...things. I should have put myself in your shoes before passing judgment on you. Once I realized that, I wanted to—"

"It's my fault," he declared fiercely, his chest heaving as he faced me, his tall stature imposing in this tiny space.

"What do you mean?"

"This." He waved his hand around the room. "It's my

fault you're here, Imogene. It's my fault you were nearly killed."

"What? No. I didn't tell you I was on my way to see you to make you feel guilty. I wanted you to know that I was sorry. That I—"

"The accident was my fault. I set the wheels in motion."

I parted my lips to argue once more, but he cut me off before I could utter a syllable.

"And not because you were on your way to see me. The man driving the car that hit you?" He drew in a long breath. "It was James Turner."

I blinked several slow blinks, my brain foggy with confusion. "I don't—"

"He was my next target. You overheard as much."

A chill ran down my spine. "I did."

"I recorded a conversation between him and Brian McGuire in Atlanta," he explained, his jaw tight. "It implicated both men in what happened to me. Then I left an anonymous tip that I saw a man matching James' description walking up to McGuire's funeral home the day before he went missing."

"But that still—"

"Last night, I attended a political fundraiser that James was also scheduled to attend. I approached him and played a snippet of the recording. Then I told him I planned to release it to the media. I just wanted him to get arrested."

"You didn't want to...take care of him yourself?"

"I wanted him to know how I felt all those years ago," he ground out, his jaw tight. "Wanted him to feel the lack of control. To wake up every day scared for his life. He was a prosecutor. Prison wouldn't be good to him." He hung his head. "I didn't think he'd make a run for it when the police showed up."

"And when he made this run..." I began.

Gideon slowly brought his red-rimmed eyes to mine. "He led police on a high-speed chase through Santa Monica, which came to an end when he crashed into your car."

He took my hand in his once more, the feel of his thumb grazing my knuckles offering me a sense of comfort.

"I've been through a lot of horrible shit, Imogene. But when I asked Henry to find out who owned the car James hit and he told me it was yours..." He pinched his lips, fighting back his emotions.

"I've never felt so damn helpless in my life. But I swear to you..."

When he returned his gaze to mine, it was full of determination and sincerity.

"I'm done with all of this. No more lies. No more revenge. No more being obsessed with the past. Instead,

I'll only look toward the future. And I hope you still want a place in that future with me. I promise to be the man you deserve. The man you fell in love with all those years ago. I'll leave all of this behind and just be Samuel Tate again. For us. Please... Forgive me, Imogene."

A wave of emotion washed over me, rendering me speechless.

Despite my conversation with Melanie, his promise to leave all of this messy business in the past was certainly a relief. But to learn he blamed himself for the accident?

He didn't force James behind the wheel of his car. Didn't make him run from the police. James made that decision for himself.

"I'm not going to do that," I told him.

He blew out a breath, hanging his head in defeat. "I understand."

"Because there's nothing to forgive."

He darted his gaze up to mine. "What do you mean? I—"

"I don't blame you for any of this."

"But it's my fault you're here. My fault you almost..."

"You can't bear the burden of this. I won't *let* you bear the burden of this. Not when James made the decision to run from the police."

"Which he never would have done if I hadn't confronted him at the fundraiser."

"I'm glad you did. You deserve closure after all the shit…" I took a moment to collect myself at the reminder of everything he'd been through.

I'd known the truth about who he was and what he endured for weeks now. Regardless, it was still difficult to think of him locked in a cage somewhere, forced to fight for his life. It was a miracle he was still alive. I wasn't going to take that for granted anymore.

"Please don't blame yourself," I finally finished once I got my emotions under control. "But if you need my forgiveness in order to move on, you have it. Just know you don't need it. There's nothing to forgive. *Nothing*."

His shoulders fell in relief and he pressed a kiss to my hand, his lips warm and soft, despite the scruff dotting his jaw. But I liked it. Liked the roughness to it. A reminder of his duplicitous nature. Rough and hard on the outside, but soft on the inside.

"Thank you, Imogene. I don't deserve it. Don't deserve you. But I swear I'll spend the rest of my life trying to prove to you that I do."

"I like the sound of that."

A wide smile tugged on his mouth, reminding me of the way Samuel once smiled. It was at complete odds with the way Gideon would smile. He didn't do it often, but when he did, it was guarded, the burden of his past preventing him from being happy. Now, it was as if that weight had lifted.

As if he was finally ready to be Samuel again.

The door to my room opened and a brunette in scrubs walked in, pulling my attention away from Gideon. "Oh, good. You're awake."

"I am."

"How are you feeling?" she asked as she checked the various monitors attached to me.

"Pretty sore."

"You've been through a lot. I want you to see the doctor and for you to try to eat something. After that, I can give you something for the pain, but it'll probably knock you out again."

"I'd rather not. Not yet anyway." I glanced toward Gideon. "I'd like to stay awake a little longer."

"You got it." She typed a few things on her tablet, then looked my way. "You have a good man there." She nodded toward Gideon. "Refused to leave your side until you woke up."

I smiled, meeting Gideon's eyes. "I do have a good man."

It was the truth. He may have done some bad things, but underneath it all, he was still a good person. And I'd do everything in my power to make him see it, too.

CHAPTER SEVEN

Gideon

The cool evening breeze circled around me, carrying the faint scent of flowers as I walked with Imogene through the garden on the roof of the hospital. Five stories below, the constant murmur and clamor of reporters buzzed like pesky gnats, an incessant reminder that my sins had drawn an audience.

I'd seen the headlines earlier this morning. *James Turner Near Death: The Rise and Fall of a Politician.* If they knew I was up here with the woman he'd almost killed, they'd have a field day.

Imogene's arm remained looped through mine as we walked slowly through the lush greenery, her movements tentative but determined.

Five days ago, I didn't know if she'd ever wake up.

Now, her collapsed lung had healed enough for the doctors to remove the chest tube — a small victory in an otherwise unfortunate situation.

She'd been getting up and walking several times a day, each step carefully monitored by nurses or me, per her doctor's orders. Today was the first time she made it all the way to the rooftop garden. It may have taken her a while, but she refused to give up.

She'd even started mild physical therapy to regain her strength, the sessions short and methodical but grueling. I'd seen the toll they took on her, but she pushed through, gritting her teeth and refusing to let me or anyone else see the worst of her pain.

That fiery spirit of hers, the one that had always drawn me to her, burned as bright as ever. It was impossible not to admire her resilience. At the same time, it gutted me to know she was enduring it all because of me.

Imogene released a soft exhale and came to a stop. She tilted her face toward the sky, a small smile forming as the last streaks of sunset painted the clouds.

"It's beautiful, isn't it?"

I followed her gaze, but found my eyes drawn back to her. Despite the bruises dotting her skin, she remained undeniably beautiful. But it wasn't just her physical appearance that captivated me. It was her strength.

"It is," I replied, unable to stop admiring her.

For a moment, the chaos of the world below felt

distant and muted. Up here, I could forget everything. My mistakes. My sins. My past. It was just Imogene and me. Like we once dreamed about all those years ago.

But then my cell buzzed in my pocket, a sharp jolt yanking me back to reality. I pulled it out, Henry's name lighting up the screen with a single message:

He's gone.

The words were small and unassuming, but their weight crashed into me with unexpected force.

James Turner was dead.

Imogene must have noticed the shift in my expression because she lightly squeezed my arm. "What is it?"

"Turner," I said evenly. "He's gone."

She didn't say anything at first, just studied me like she was trying to decipher my reaction. We had known this was an inevitability. But now it was real. The man who arranged to sell me had drawn his final breath. The man who had Jonah beat so badly he became brain dead was no longer alive.

"How do you feel?" Imogene asked softly, concern swirling in her dark eyes.

How did I feel? I wasn't sure how to answer.

It was bittersweet, a hollow victory.

A part of me wanted to revel in his death. In the fact that he could no longer harm anyone else. But another part couldn't help but feel that his death was too quick, too clean, too easy.

A few days ago, all I could think about was making him suffer like I had. I wanted him to wake up every morning worried he may not survive the day. Wanted him to live in fear of what he may endure during his waking hours.

Those thoughts had brought me to this point — to nearly losing Imogene. I couldn't go back there. *Wouldn't* go back there.

Never again.

"He got what he deserved," I declared firmly.

She didn't look convinced. "You're not upset it didn't happen the way you hoped?"

"I told you when you woke up. I'm done with all of that."

Her eyes stayed on mine, searching for cracks. For any hint I wasn't being completely honest with her.

"What about Liam?" she asked quietly.

My chest tightened at the mention of his name. The man who had set it all in motion. The man who I thought was a friend, then betrayed me in a way I never anticipated.

"You're really okay with walking away? With him getting away with everything?"

I shifted my gaze from her, focusing on the horizon. For a long moment, I didn't answer. I didn't know if I *was* okay. I hated Liam with every fiber of my being. Hated the idea of him not suffering the consequences of his actions.

But I hated the person I became in my pursuit of revenge even more, especially as I raked my eyes over Imogene's battered frame, bruises marring her fair skin, her arm in a sling.

"I have to be," I said with determination, locking my gaze with hers. "I lost sight of what's important. That's you, Imogene." I pressed a hand to her cheek, relishing in her soft skin. "We have each other again. No more living in the past. No more playing god. I just want to live for you. For us."

"For us," she echoed, and for a moment, the weight on my chest eased.

I bent down to press a kiss to her forehead, letting the warmth of her presence chase away the darkness. The world around us disappeared, the noise below forgotten, the memories of revenge fading into distant echoes.

Exactly where they belonged.

Behind me.

In my past.

They had no place in my present or my future.

Not anymore.

CHAPTER EIGHT

Imogene

The sun had begun to set on my ninth day stuck in this hospital when a knock sounded on my door during a rare moment to myself.

Between Gideon being glued to my side, as well as my parents and Melanie visiting me as much as possible, I'd barely had any time to be alone and reflect on everything that had happened. From the accident, to Gideon's admission, and then his promise that he was done being Gideon Saint.

I still wasn't sure how I felt about that. I hadn't had *time* to figure out how I felt about that.

But Gideon just left to attend to some business down in San Diego, allowing me some much-needed alone time. The last thing I wanted was more visitors.

I had a feeling I wasn't going to get my wish, though.

"I'm sorry to interrupt," one of my nurses said as she popped her head into my room.

"Is anything wrong?" I asked, hoping my most recent round of tests and scans came back clear.

I'd been on the mend for over week now, but the doctors still wanted to keep me in the hospital for a bit longer to make sure there weren't any complications from my surgery. So far, there hadn't been. As long as I continued to make positive progress, I'd be released in just a few more days. I was itching to get out of this place.

"Not at all. There's someone from the FBI here who'd like to ask you a few questions. I can tell him you're not up to it yet, if you'd prefer."

I let out a heavy sigh.

With Liam still missing after having withdrawn large sums of money from his various accounts, I knew it was only a matter of time before law enforcement came knocking on my door, considering my once close ties to him.

I prayed their investigation didn't also lead to Gideon... Samuel.

"It's okay."

"I'm happy to send him away," the nurse said, obviously picking up on my reluctance.

"It's fine," I assured her.

"Okay." She turned and disappeared down the hallway.

I closed my eyes and took a deep breath to calm my nerves. I told myself it would be okay. That I hadn't done anything wrong. But I couldn't help but feel anxious about what questions he might ask.

"Ms. Prescott?"

I snapped my eyes open to see a tall man standing in the doorway. Everything about him screamed law enforcement. From the dark suit, to his perfectly groomed silver hair and shaven jawline, to his no-nonsense demeanor. I got the feeling this was a guy who took his job seriously.

"I'm Agent Myers with the FBI."

"Pleasure to meet you," I replied with a congenial smile.

"May I sit down?" He gestured to the chair beside my bed.

"Of course."

"Thank you." He walked across the room and sat in the chair, his eyes focused on me with every step.

It was unnerving.

"What can I help you with today, Agent Myers?" I asked, trying to keep my tone friendly and composed.

"I'm investigating a cold case in Georgia that appears to be connected to recent criminal activity, both in Georgia and here in California."

"Okay," I drew out, my anxiety increasing with every second. The air in the room suddenly felt heavy and oppressive, as if it were holding its breath, waiting for whatever question he was about to ask.

Much like I was.

"When was the last time you saw William Pierce?"

It took me a moment to figure out he was referring to Liam. I hadn't heard anyone call him William in years.

"About three weeks ago. He stopped by my townhouse."

"What did you discuss?"

"We'd gotten into an argument a week prior, and he came over to apologize."

"What was the argument about?"

"He doesn't approve of my current choice in romantic partner."

Agent Myers arched a brow. "Gideon Saint?"

I swallowed hard, wondering how he knew of my relationship with him. In all actuality, we'd only spent a handful of nights together. Yet, this FBI agent knew about us.

How?

And why did he seem so interested in my response?

"Yes," I finally answered, keeping my expression even.

"And you haven't seen or spoken to Mr. Pierce since that day?"

"No."

"Did he say anything else when he came to see you? No matter how insignificant, it could be helpful."

"He did mention he was heading out of town that night and wouldn't be back for a few days," I offered, hoping that was enough to satisfy him.

"Nothing else?"

"I'm sorry," I offered, then furrowed my brow, feigning confusion. "What's all of this about?"

He pushed out a long sigh. "I'm sure you're already aware, but over a week ago, a recording was leaked to the media. This recording was of a conversation between James Turner and a funeral director in Atlanta, Brian McGuire, where they discussed their roles in the botched coverup of the murder of Samuel Tate. In that same recording, they referred to a third person who actually pulled the trigger but was never named. I believe that person was William Pierce, considering he had the most to gain from Mr. Tate's death."

I swallowed hard, my heart heavy at the reminder of how wrong I'd been about Liam. It still made my stomach churn to know I allowed him to comfort me, all while he was the one who'd wanted Samuel dead.

"Turner was already a person of interest in McGuire's disappearance, thanks to an anonymous tip Atlanta PD received. It's our theory that Mr. Pierce saw the temperature rising and decided to make a run for it.

So far, we haven't been able to track him down. Phone records have come up empty. Same for bank records. I was hoping you might have spoken to him recently. Or at least know somewhere he might go if he wanted to lie low for a bit. You two have been pretty close for quite some time."

"I assume you've already checked his various homes here in California, as well as in Atlanta, Chicago, New York, and London."

"We have."

"I don't know where else he might go. We've sort of grown apart over the past few years. Since Samuel Tate's death, I suppose."

He nodded, his penetrating gaze studying me for several anxiety-inducing moments. "You don't seem surprised at the idea that William Pierce could be responsible for what happened to Mr. Tate. In fact, you barely reacted, as if you already knew of the role he played in all of this."

My face heated, my mouth growing dry. "I guess I saw how money and success affected him. He's not the same person he was when we first met, which is why we're not as close as we once were."

He didn't immediately say anything, simply studying me with even more scrutiny. Every other sound in the room seemed amplified — my unsteady breathing, the tapping of my nails against the bed railing, even the rustling of my hospital gown. I feared the longer he stayed, the more he'd realize the truth.

"I wish I could be more helpful," I said with a smile, hoping he'd take the hint and leave. "But I just don't know where Liam could be."

Time seemed to stand still as he continued studying me with an intense, unwavering gaze. His piercing dark eyes bore into mine, making me feel like he could see right through me. I understood why he made such a good cop. Hell, after mere minutes in his presence, I was ready to confess every bad thing I'd ever done.

Finally, he gave a subtle nod, as if in approval of my response. He stood and reached into the inside pocket of his suit jacket.

"If you think of anything else or if he contacts you in any way, give me a call." He handed me a business card.

I took it, relieved he hadn't pressed too much about Gideon Saint or Samuel Tate.

But just as he was about to open the door, he unexpectedly turned around again.

"Do you mind if I ask one more question?"

My stomach twisted with unease over what that might be.

"Of course." I gritted out.

"When was the last time you saw Samuel Tate?"

"S-Samuel Tate?" I repeated, my heart rate kicking up, the tiny hairs all over my body standing on end.

"It's my understanding you two were good friends before what happened to him."

I nodded slightly. "We were."

"So when was the last time you saw him?"

I shook my head, desperately trying to buy myself some time and hoping he wouldn't sense any deceit in my words.

"The day he died. Or that I was made to believe he died." I furrowed my brow. "Why do you ask?"

"It's just a theory I've been working on."

"A theory?"

"My gut tells me this entire scenario isn't as clear cut as some of the evidence suggests."

"It doesn't?"

"No."

He took a few steps back into the room, but didn't sit down. Still, his presence seemed to fill the space, suffocating me and reminding me what was at stake.

"When I started looking at the big picture, a few things stood out. Starting with you being sent those necklaces, then being attacked in the alley."

His words hung heavy in the air, each one landing with a thud and leaving me reeling. I tried to maintain my composure, flashing a poker face I'd perfected all those years ago while living with my sperm donor. But as he continued reciting off all the suspicious events, I felt it slip.

"Approximately two weeks later, a body was found on Mr. Pierce's boat that belonged to the man who'd given you the necklace in the club, Benjamin Astor. Then less than a week later, Alton Sinclair was found dead of a supposed self-inflicted gunshot wound to the head, and a glass containing Samuel Tate's fingerprints was found at the scene. Just a few days after that, James Turner paid Brian McGuire a visit in Atlanta, who then turned up missing. Then just a few weeks later, a recording of their conversation was released, which would have resulted in Turner's arrest, had he not attempted to flee from the cops."

As he leveled his stare on me, my heart pounded in my chest, making me think it was about to burst out of my body.

"And your theory is?" I prodded, despite every voice in my head telling me to put an end to this conversation right now.

"That maybe these recent deaths aren't simply attempts to cover up what happened all those years ago, but are acts of revenge. By Samuel Tate himself."

"But he's dead," I protested, surprised at how convincing I sounded. Hell, if I didn't know any better, I would have believed me.

But I knew better.

"We don't know that," Agent Myers argued. "In the recording, Brian McGuire confessed to selling Mr. Tate.

He could have survived and escaped, and is now getting back at everyone who he believes wronged him. Alton Sinclair. James Turner. Brian McGuire. Now with William Pierce having essentially disappeared, it's possible he's also eliminated him. Which means you're the last name on his hit list to cross off. Hell, the necklaces and the attack in the alley could have been his first attempt at doing just that."

"That sounds a little far-fetched," I said, praying my voice didn't sound as nervous as I felt right now. "Like something out of a movie."

"My boss said the same thing, considering the only proof we have that Samuel Tate is still alive is a single fingerprint, which could very easily be several years old." He arched a single brow, his unnerving gaze locked on mine, as if looking for the slightest indication I might believe him.

Agent Myers seemed determined to get a reaction out of me, waiting for me to slip up and reveal something incriminating.

"Samuel Tate was the kindest, most gentle person I knew," I declared with vindication. "He wouldn't hurt anyone. Not like you're suggesting. And he certainly wouldn't hurt me."

"You'd be surprised what people are capable of when they're pushed to their limits."

I didn't respond. Just glared at him.

I expected him to turn and leave, but he didn't. Instead, he stated, "It's my understanding Gideon Saint is the one who came to your rescue that night in the alley."

"What does that have to do with everything?"

He raked his scrutinizing stare over me once more. "I'm not sure yet." He smirked. "Good day, Ms. Prescott."

With one last look, he turned around and disappeared into the hallway, leaving me on edge and making me regret ever agreeing to answer his questions.

CHAPTER NINE

Imogene

"You must be happy to be breaking out of here," Mom said as she folded some of the clothes Henry had brought to me from my townhouse at the beginning of my hospital stay.

After two long weeks, my doctors had finally cleared me to go back to San Diego. As grateful as I was for everything the staff here did to save my life, I was looking forward to being somewhere other than this damn hospital. Somewhere peaceful.

Somewhere that I wasn't woken up every few hours to have my vitals checked yet again.

"I'm definitely ready for life to return to normal." I gritted a smile. "Or as normal as possible, all things considered." I gave her a knowing look. "Are you sure you and Lachlan don't want to come down to San Diego?"

"We'll be back to check on you soon, but we thought it was better if we gave you some time to get settled in with Gideon." She winced slightly. "Samuel. I'm not really sure what to call him." She laughed under her breath.

"I'm not sure, either," I admitted honestly. "All things considered, it's probably best to stick to Gideon." I fidgeted with the hem of my shirt, growing uneasy as I recalled my conversation with Agent Myers several days ago.

I hadn't told Gideon or my parents about it. I didn't know what to say. I convinced myself nothing would come of Myers' so-called "theory". Or maybe I simply *hoped* nothing would come of it. After all, he didn't have any proof to back up his assertions.

For all intents and purposes, Samuel Tate was dead. Agent Myers said it himself. The only proof he had that Samuel Tate might still be alive was his fingerprints on the glass at Alton Sinclair's cabin that could have been left there several years ago.

But something about Agent Myers made me think he could be a problem.

"How are you doing with...everything?" Mom asked, pulling my attention back to her.

Despite the fact that my parents had been here every

day since the accident, this was the first time I had any meaningful alone time with my mom. Typically, either Lachlan or Gideon was also around. Especially Gideon. While I understood the guilt he felt over the accident and his need to prove himself to me, his constant presence had been somewhat suffocating.

But right now, it was just my mom and me. I had a feeling she sensed I needed this time with her before she returned to Atlanta.

"I have Samuel back." I forced a smile. "Why wouldn't I be happy about that?"

"I still can't believe it. You told me about your suspicions, but I didn't think it was possible."

"You and me both."

She gave me an understanding smile before her expression turned serious. "But is it Samuel you want?" She set the last t-shirt inside my duffel bag, then sat in the chair beside my wheelchair. "Or Gideon?"

I parted my lips, but hesitated, not immediately answering. It shouldn't have even been a question in my mind.

For years, I would have given anything to have Samuel back. I finally did. And not only in body, but also in spirit. Since the accident, Gideon had been like a different person. Like Samuel again.

Just like I wanted.

Then why did it feel like something was missing?

"I love Samuel," I finally said.

It was the only truthful thing I could muster. But it didn't escape my mother's notice that I failed to actually answer the question.

"Regardless of the things he may have done, Gideon was still a good person, Imogene," she encouraged softly. "Maybe over the next few weeks, you can help him see that."

I nodded, but didn't say anything, ruminating her words over in my mind for several moments until the door opened and Lachlan and Gideon walked in.

But he didn't look like Gideon anymore.

He didn't look like Samuel, either. Not really. He was dressed more casually than he typically did, wearing dark jeans and a button-down shirt with the sleeves rolled up. It almost felt like he was trying to be Samuel again but didn't know how.

"Are you ready to go?" he asked softly.

I gave him an overly enthusiastic smile, hoping to hide any disappointment or confusion. "Definitely."

"I'm glad you're feeling better, kid." Lachlan gave me a gentle hug, pressing a kiss to my temple.

"Thanks for being here."

"Anything for you. You know that."

I met his eyes. He may not have been my father by blood, but since he walked into my mother's life all those years ago, he filled the role of my father in a way my sperm donor never had.

"I do."

"We'll be out to visit soon."

"Looking forward to it."

He gave me one last hug, then turned toward Gideon. "You'll take good care of my girl."

It wasn't a question. More like a statement. Or a demand.

Gideon gave him a curt nod and extended his hand. "Imogene is my priority. Nothing else."

Lachlan took his hand, and the two men embraced briefly in a bro-hug.

"Call if you need anything," Mom chimed in, leaning down to give me a tight squeeze. "Or if you just want to talk."

"I will," I promised her.

"And don't push yourself too hard," she added sternly. "I know you want to get back to normal as soon as possible, but it'll take some time."

"Yes, Mom," I playfully groaned, but I couldn't fault her.

Even though I routinely warned my patients not to overdo it because it could sometimes cause more harm than good, I wanted to get back on my feet as quick as possible.

Wanted to put this chapter of my life behind me and only look toward my future.

But was it a future with Gideon?

Or Samuel?

"I'll make sure she doesn't overdo it," Gideon assured her.

"Thank you."

He gave her a brief hug and kiss, then looked my way. "Are you ready?" he asked again.

"Yes."

He moved behind my wheelchair and pushed me into the hallway, where a nurse stepped in to take over.

To my surprise, several security guards were also waiting.

"What's going on?" I asked Gideon, confused about why we were heading in a different direction from the elevator. "Where are we going?"

"To the loading docks. A car is waiting for us there."

"Why?"

"Reporters are still camped in front of the hospital. Everyone's hoping to get a soundbite from the woman who was nearly killed by a U.S. Senator."

There was a sharp edge to his voice, and I could sense his frustration. "You'll need to put this on." He pulled a baseball cap out of a shopping bag.

"A Dodgers hat?" I eyed it warily. "In case you've forgotten, I'm an Atlanta fan."

"As am I. But I can't send you out there wearing a hat with their logo. It'll be a dead giveaway it's you. You can take it off once we're on the freeway."

"Fine," I huffed, reluctantly putting on the hat as the nurse pushed me into the freight elevator.

When we reached the basement, the doors opened and the nurse wheeled me toward a pair of open double doors, even more security guards lingering nearby. I wasn't sure this much security presence was necessary, but if I'd learned anything during my time with Gideon, it was that he didn't take my safety lightly.

Still, this all seemed like overkill. Was there something more going on than just keeping reporters at bay?

As we approached an idling black SUV, Henry jumped out and opened the back door, giving my arm a small squeeze before getting in behind the wheel once more. Gideon helped me stand, keeping me steady as I climbed into the back seat. He placed a blanket over my stomach before pulling the seatbelt across my torso.

The second Gideon slid in beside me, Henry put the car into drive and pulled away from the loading dock.

As we passed the front of the hospital, it quickly became clear why Gideon insisted we leave through the loading dock. Dozens upon dozens of reporters swarmed the area, vultures ready to pounce on anyone who looked remotely like me.

"What do they want?" I mumbled partly to myself.

"What most reporters do these days," Gideon ground out, his jaw tight. "To capitalize on what happened to you, all to increase their ratings and hopefully make them more money. But don't worry about them..." He grabbed my hand and brought it to his lips, giving me a reassuring kiss. "Right now, your only focus should be on regaining your strength."

"Thank you." I leaned my head back against the headrest, exhausted from days of interrupted sleep.

"Of course." He pressed one more kiss to my hand, then lowered it, but didn't let go.

Instead, the soft brush of his thumb along my knuckles offered me comfort as I closed my eyes, settling in for the drive.

But after what felt like only minutes, the car came to a stop and Gideon gently nudged me awake.

"We're here."

I fluttered my eyes open, expecting to be at his house in San Diego. But we were in front of a building adjacent to an airstrip, the lights of the runway visible in the distance.

"Where are we?" I asked.

"A private terminal near the airport."

"What are we doing here?"

"Going home." He flashed me a smile, then slid out of the SUV, rushing around to open my door for me. "Are you okay to walk a few steps?" he asked as a man hurried toward us with a luggage cart and began unloading our bags at Henry's instruction. "The plane's ready and waiting for us."

"A private plane?" I playfully waggled my brows, taking Gideon's outstretched hand and allowing him to help me to my feet. "You sure know how to spoil a girl."

"And I intend on spoiling you every day for the rest of your life. If you'll let me."

"How can I say no to that?"

He brushed a gentle kiss to my lips before pulling back and meeting Henry's gaze. "Thanks, brother. For everything."

Something unspoken passed between the two men in the few silent seconds before Gideon wrapped him in a brief hug. When he released him, Henry turned his attention toward me.

"Take care of yourself. And him."

I laughed under my breath as he gave me a gentle squeeze. "I'm pretty sure he can take care of himself."

"Maybe. Just don't let him lose sight of who he is," he whispered before dropping his hold on me.

"Ready?" Gideon asked, touching a hand to my back.

"Let's go home."

"I like the sound of that." He beamed a wide smile that reminded me so much of Samuel.

I should have been thrilled.

Instead, it only made me long for the mysterious stranger in black who I watched kill a man with his bare hands.

CHAPTER TEN

Gideon

"Where are we going?" Imogene asked as I drove north along the freeway after landing at a private terminal by San Diego airport.

Normally, I wouldn't go through the trouble of flying from LA to San Diego when the drive typically only took a little more than two hours, depending on traffic.

But I wanted Imogene to be taken care of.

Despite the fact that she was getting better every day, she still struggled to get comfortable in a sitting position due to the injuries to her ribs. To ask her to be in pain for over two hours? I wasn't going to do that. So I hired a private plane to fly us the hundred or so miles down the coast.

"I thought we were going home," she continued.

"We are," I said evenly, keeping my eyes on the road.

"But we just passed the exit for La Jolla."

"I can't take you to your place right now, Imogene." I stole a glance at her to gauge her reaction. "There are reporters camped outside."

"What about your house?"

"I don't think that's a good idea, either. All things considered, I think we both deserve a fresh start. That's where I'm taking you. To what I hope can be our fresh start."

"Fresh start," she repeated, as if testing the words on her tongue. Then she reached across the center console, linking her fingers with mine. "I like the sound of that."

"Me, too," I murmured, bringing her hand to my lips, savoring in the feel of her skin.

I'd never take it for granted again. Not after those few harrowing hours when I wasn't sure if I'd ever feel her warmth. Hear her voice. Taste her lips.

This was my second chance. I was going to do what I should have done months ago. I was going to stop living in the past and only worry about moving forward.

We drove in an easy silence up toward Del Mar, and I navigated to the gated community where Henry found the perfect beach bungalow for Imogene and me to live, at least for now. I'd only been here once, and only after Henry already bought it. I trusted his judgment, and he certainly delivered, especially as I led

Imogene inside and her eyes widened at her surroundings.

The bungalow was one story, which was exactly what she needed right now. The open kitchen and dining room flowed seamlessly into the living room, the far wall made up of sliding glass doors with a stunning view of the Pacific Ocean. While it was much smaller than the house I'd been living in, I much preferred this place. It had more charm and personality instead of being some huge monstrosity built on the shore. The only reason I bought the other house was because Liam had hoped to buy it.

But now that I was buying somewhere with Imogene in mind, I wanted it to be something she'd like.

Somewhere she could imagine living the rest of her life.

Somewhere like we once dreamed of building together.

"Do you want to see the bedroom?" I asked as she took in the soothing blue and gray tones of the living room.

"That would be great."

"This way." I led her down a hallway just off the foyer, steering her to the last door on the left. "It's not nearly as big as the primary bedroom in my other house, but it still has a great view of the ocean."

"It definitely does," she said as she padded across the

room and toward the French doors that opened onto the back patio.

"I had Henry bring a bunch of your things from your townhouse here, but if you're missing something, make a list and I'll grab it for you. Is there anything you need right now?"

She faced me. "Actually, now that my doctor has cleared me, I'd love to take a bath and wash my hair. Wash the hospital off me, if at all possible."

"Right. The bathroom's in here." I moved toward the open door and flicked on the light, illuminating the space.

While it wasn't as massive as the ensuite bathroom at the other house, it was just as opulent. Smooth marble vanity countertops gleamed under the warm lighting. An oversized shower with multiple shower heads beckoned from one side of the room, while a luxurious jetted tub awaited on the other.

"That tub looks like heaven," she sighed. "You have no idea how much I've been looking forward to finally having a bath, especially now that my incisions have healed enough for me to do so."

"I'll give you some privacy then." I started to turn, but her voice stopped me.

"Actually..." She trailed off, her frustration evident in the lines of her face.

"What is it?"

"It's just..." She worried her bottom lip. "I haven't been able to wash my hair in over a week. It hurt too much to lift my arms over my head. Still does. I..."

"You need help," I stated, finishing her thought.

"I'm sorry." She apologized sheepishly.

I touched her chin, forcing her gaze back to mine. "You have nothing to apologize for."

"I just hate feeling like a burden."

"You could never be a burden," I assured her, pressing a tender kiss to her mouth. "Plus, a beautiful woman is asking me to take a bath with her? I'd be a fool to say no."

She pinched her lips together, her playful side returning. "I don't recall asking you to join me. Just for some help washing my hair. You don't need to be in the tub to do that."

"Is that what you want? To bathe alone?"

"Since you're offering, I'd be remiss to pass up the opportunity." She hoisted herself onto her toes, her lips brushing against mine.

It was an innocent gesture, but between the heat of her breath and her sultry tone, my cock was throbbing in my jeans.

It didn't help that it had been weeks since I'd allowed myself to feel any sort of pleasure, even at my own hands. I wasn't sure how I was going to handle being in the tub with Imogene, feeling her naked skin against mine, without wanting to sink inside of her.

But as I removed her sling and carefully helped to lift her t-shirt over her head, all desire immediately vanished as my eyes fell on her bruised and scarred stomach.

Not because I found her hideous. That wasn't the case at all.

This was the first time I'd seen the consequences of the car accident that nearly took her life.

The car accident I had a hand in, despite everyone's insistence to the contrary.

Despite *Imogene's* insistence to the contrary.

Now that I was seeing the patchwork of bruises still prominent against her pale flesh, even two weeks later, it took everything I had not to break down.

She clutched my cheeks, forcing my gaze toward hers. "It is not your fault," she declared for what felt like the thousandth time since she woke up. "Say it."

"What?"

"Say it, Gideon. Say 'it's not my fault.'"

I parted my lips and shook my head. "I can't. I—"

"For me. Say it for me," she pleaded, her grip on my face tightening ever so slightly. "Because I can't stand the idea that you're going to keep burdening yourself with this."

I attempted to protest again, but she cut me off.

"Please. For me."

Her eyes practically begged for me to give her this. I didn't want to. Didn't want to do anything that would make her think I didn't hold myself responsible. But it was impossible to deny her when she looked at me like this.

"It's not my fault," I finally conceded, each word a fight.

"There." She beamed, her smile nearly stealing my breath. "That wasn't so hard, was it?"

"If I'm being honest, it was."

"Then I'll make you say that every day until you finally believe it." She left a soft kiss on my cheek before heading toward the tub, turning on the water and adjusting the temperature until it was just right.

All I could do was marvel at how resilient she was. It shouldn't have surprised me. It was one of the things that attracted me to her in the beginning. And it made me fall even more in love with her now.

After helping her out of her sweatpants, doing my best to keep my reaction to the rest of her bruises to myself, I held her steady as she climbed into the tub. Then I quickly discarded my clothes before sliding in behind her.

Reaching for the handheld shower nozzle, I turned it on and tested the temperature before running it over Imogene's hair.

"Is the water okay?" I asked.

"It's perfect."

"Good."

Once her hair was wet enough, I reached for her shampoo and squirt a little into my hands. Then I massaged it into her scalp, relishing in the familiar scent. She closed her eyes, her breathing soft and even as she melted into my touch.

"I'm sorry you have to do this," she attempted to apologize again.

"Don't apologize, Imogene." I forced her stare toward mine, wanting her to see the truth in my words. "I want to be here. Want to take care of you. I love you." I dipped my lips closer. "Unconditionally."

"Unconditionally," she repeated as I pressed my mouth against hers.

As my tongue swiped against hers in my first real taste of her since the accident, I could practically feel the pieces of us sliding back together.

The old us.

When I first decided to walk away from my plan of revenge, I wasn't sure what I was going to do. What my purpose in life would be.

Now I knew.

My purpose was Imogene. Taking care of her. Loving her unconditionally.

Like we promised all those years ago.

CHAPTER ELEVEN

Gideon

"Are you comfortable?" Gideon asked after arranging all the pillows around me so I could sleep on my good side.

As I settled in, the soft warmth of the duvet enveloped me and I let out a contented sigh.

"This is infinitely better than that hospital bed. I hate sleeping on my back."

"I know," he chuckled as he slid under the covers beside me. He shifted onto his side to face me, his deep blue eyes sparkling in the dim light.

This wasn't the first time we'd shared a bed together, but it felt different. I wasn't sure what to make of it. He had Samuel's personality, for the most part. But he had Gideon's face and body.

And scars.

At least in my mind they were Gideon's scars.

I tried to tell myself I'd eventually get used to it. That this new dynamic would take some adjusting for both of us. At some point, I'd eventually forget about Gideon Saint and the things he'd done.

But did I *want* to forget him? His passion? His darkness?

"Are *you* comfortable?" I asked as he gingerly ran his hand along my arm, his caress nothing like the way Gideon touched me, possessive and in control.

"Why do you ask?"

I parted my lips, but quickly clamped them shut.

It didn't dawn on me until now that I'd never mentioned stumbling on that closet in his old home. In the turmoil of coming to terms not only with the fact that he was Samuel, but also that the man I loved was a killer, it hadn't crossed my mind.

But I didn't want to brush it aside any longer. I wanted to know more. Wanted to know all the pieces that made up the man he was now.

Maybe it would help me find some clarity between the two opposing sides of his personality.

"I found the closet in your house. I wasn't snooping or anything," I added quickly when I noticed his expression change, his muscles going rigid. "I went looking for you. But when I walked into what I thought was your room, I saw the closet. If it can even be called a closet. Most closets have flooring and walls. They're not stripped down to the studs."

He pulled away, rolling onto his back and staring at the ceiling. I couldn't help but feel a pang of guilt for bringing up what was obviously a sensitive subject.

But that didn't stop me from pressing on, despite his silence.

"Is that where you usually slept?" I ran a lithe finger along one of the many scars dotting his chest.

"It is."

"Why?"

He glanced my way, briefly hesitating. Then he pushed out a long sigh.

"After sleeping on the ground for years, I'd grown accustomed to it." He scooped my hand in his and pressed a soft kiss to it. "It wasn't until I spent the night with you in Pebble Beach that I felt comfortable in a bed again."

I swallowed hard, my heart aching at what he'd endured, even if I didn't know most of the details. But I *wanted* to know the details.

Wanted to know everything.

"What was it like?"

"Spending the night with you?" He faced me and hovered his lips over mine, sending a thrill through me. "Heaven."

His mouth moved against mine in a tender kiss.

Just when I started to deepen it, he pulled back, as if consciously not wanting to get me worked up. It was killing me that we couldn't be intimate. Maybe then I wouldn't be confused about what to think about this new version of Gideon. Maybe I just needed that connection again. A reminder of who we were to each other.

"That's not what I mean." I gave him a knowing look before lowering my voice. "I'm talking about where you were. Where they kept you. What was it like?"

He stared at me for several long moments, and I braced myself to hear the worst of humanity. To listen to his suffering, his pain, his torment.

Instead, he released a slow breath and shook his head, leaning toward me and touching a tender kiss to my forehead. It was such a Samuel thing to do. Not something Gideon Saint would.

"It doesn't matter." He cupped my face with his calloused hands. "I made you a promise at the hospital. And I intend on keeping that promise. No more looking back." He inched his mouth toward mine once more. "Only looking forward."

"I appreciate that." I ran my fingers through his dark hair. "But I don't want you to feel like you can't talk about it. I want to know that part of you. Like it or not, what you went through will always be a part of who you are. The man you were will always be a part of who you are." I erased the last bit of space between us, my lips brushing with his. "Gideon Saint will always be a part of who you are."

"No, Imogene. He's not." His expression was even, devoid of even a hint of the passion and fever I'd grown accustomed to from this man.

From this face.

"Gideon Saint is gone. It's just me. Just Samuel." He pulled me into his arms, and I listened to the steady thumping of his heart. "*Your* Samuel."

"My Samuel," I repeated, although my words lacked even a hint of enthusiasm.

I should have been content with his desire to put the past behind him. If anyone would understand wanting to do that, it was me. Hell, I'd moved across the country so I could do just that.

But hearing him say that Gideon Saint was gone?

My heart broke at the thought.

It was like I was in love with two completely different men, even though they shared the same body. But was I actually in love with Samuel Tate after all this time?

Or was I just in love with the idea of him?

CHAPTER TWELVE

Imogene

My eyes fluttered open to rays of sun streaming in through the blinds, casting a warm glow across the space. I took a moment to adjust to my surroundings, my peaceful and quaint new home a stark contrast to the sterile hospital room I'd called home for the past two weeks.

I stretched in the luxurious bed before shifting onto my side, expecting to see Gideon next to me. Instead, his side of the bed was empty.

It reminded me of the morning a few weeks ago when I woke up in his house after what I thought was a breakthrough. I thought I'd finally reached him, cut through the iron walls he'd built up after everything he'd endured.

I thought we could be whole again.

Thought we could be *us* again.

Now we were.

So why did it feel...wrong?

I quickly pushed away the thought and slid out of bed, wincing slightly as I found my footing. Then I padded on light feet down the hallway, the smell of coffee like a beacon.

As I entered the kitchen, I couldn't help but smile at the sight that greeted me. Gideon stood at the stove, his broad shoulders relaxed as he flipped bacon in the skillet. His hair was disheveled and a pair of gray sweatpants hung from his hips, revealing the intricate pattern of scars that dotted his toned torso.

Scars he once tried to hide.

Now he wore them like a badge.

Just like I wore mine.

As if sensing my gaze on him, he glanced over his shoulder and met my eyes with a warm smile that lit up his entire face.

"Morning," he murmured as he approached me, brushing his lips against mine in a gentle kiss. "How did you sleep?"

"Amazing. It was so quiet and peaceful."

"Are you hungry? I can whip up a frittata if you'd like. Or something else."

"A frittata?"

He nodded, a hint of amusement sparkling in his eyes. "Like you taught me all those years ago."

"It's one of my favorite memories," I admitted. "Or perhaps I should say what happened *after* I showed you how to make a frittata is one of my favorite memories." I smirked.

"Is that right?" He waggled his brows, his pupils flaming with lust.

"Most definitely."

One of the first mornings we spent together, I'd woken up to surprise him with breakfast. At the time, he was more of a night owl, since it was the only time he had to work on his gaming platform with Liam.

But when he walked into the kitchen and saw me cooking, he asked me to teach him so *he* could make *me* breakfast.

Except neither one of us was able to keep our hands off each other, to the point that he hauled me onto the kitchen island and made me see stars.

The frittata definitely came out overcooked.

But true to his word, the next time he stayed over, I woke up to the delicious smell of bacon and eggs. And every morning we spent together after that, he continued to make me breakfast... Until I woke up one morning to that devastating phone call.

"How long did the doctor say we had to wait?" he groaned, his frustration evident.

"A few more weeks. But that doesn't mean we can't do other things." I gave him a coy look as I ran my fingers down his stomach.

But before I could slip my hand underneath the waistband of his sweatpants, he scooped it up in his, brushing a soft kiss along my knuckles.

"You have no idea how much I'd love to do other things, but I want you to heal first. I don't want to do anything that could cause you even more pain."

"You should know by now that I like a little pain." I dragged my body closer to his, desperate for a taste of the passion and fervor I craved.

"That I do." His eyes darkened, and he covered my lips with his. But just as I started to deepen the exchange, he pulled away. "This is important to me. I want you to give yourself and your body the time it needs to recover."

I frowned, swallowing hard through the lump forming in my throat.

Sensing my obvious disappointment, he looped an arm around my waist and dragged me flush against him. He dipped his head into the crook of my neck, his breath hot on my skin.

"Enjoy your rest, Imogene. The second the doctor gives you the all clear to resume regular activity, I plan on making up for lost time to the point that you'll be walking bowlegged for days." When he met my gaze, I caught a mischievous glint within. "If you can walk at all."

I bit my lower lip to fight against the smile begging to be set free. "I like the sound of that."

"Me, too." He captured my mouth, his tongue briefly swiping against mine. "Why don't you go sit on the terrace while I make you some breakfast? After being cooped up in that hospital, I'm sure you could use some fresh air and vitamin D."

"I definitely could," I agreed, allowing him to guide me toward the sliding glass doors off the living room.

As he helped me settle into one of the plush lounge chairs, I couldn't help but feel grateful for this moment of peace. The sun shone brightly down on the ocean waves, causing them to glimmer, everything about my surroundings picturesque.

I'd always loved being near the water, especially once my mom met Lachlan and he taught me to surf. I may not have been all that good at it, but whenever I was out on the water, when it was just me and the ocean, I was able to clear my mind.

Figure out what was important.

"You'll be back on your board soon enough," Gideon said, able to read my thoughts. "For now, I hope living mere feet from the ocean is enough."

"It's more than enough," I assured him.

"I'll be back soon with breakfast."

He left a gentle kiss on my lips, then disappeared inside.

I relaxed into my lounge chair, basking in the feel of the sun warming my face, drawing in a deep breath of the salty sea air. This was perfect.

As much as I thought it excessive for him to buy a house in Del Mar when he already had a stunning home just down the shore in La Jolla, I now understood his reasoning. This house represented a fresh start, a clean slate for us to build a future together that wasn't tainted by lies or betrayal. Something we both deserved after everything.

"Here we are." Gideon's deep voice pulled my eyes from the water and toward him as he set a tray containing a few plates on the small table between us. "Spinach, mushroom, and feta frittata with bacon. Because someone once told me that bacon makes everything better." He flashed me a wink.

"Sounds like a pretty smart person."

"Most definitely."

I grabbed the fork and sliced into the frittata, bringing it up to my mouth, biting back my moan at the first taste of real food in two weeks.

"I hope you like it. It's been a few years since I've made breakfast for anyone. Or really cooked at all."

"It's like riding a bike," I said through a tight smile, pushing down the reminder of precisely why he hadn't cooked in so long. "You never really forget. And it's perfect. Just like I remember."

A gentle smile crossed his face as he reached for the folded newspaper on the breakfast tray. Opening it to a page toward the back, he set it on the table between us without saying another word.

He didn't have to.

After all, this was once our morning routine — coffee, breakfast, and a crossword puzzle. They were some of my favorite memories of Samuel.

While I loved the connection I experienced whenever we made love, there was something about the quiet moments spent together as we ruminated over the various clues that felt even more intimate.

Maybe this was what I needed in order to push away my uncertainty. A reminder of what made us...us.

I picked up a piece of bacon and took a bite, leaning close and scanning the first clue.

"Mythical bird reborn from the ashes," he read.

"Phoenix," we both answered at the same time, then broke out into laughter.

As we ate breakfast and worked on the crossword puzzle, we fell into an easy rhythm, laughing over clues, playfully arguing when we disagreed on an answer. It was so easy, as though no time had passed and nothing had changed.

But things *had* changed. I couldn't shake the shadow

of Gideon Saint looming in the back of my mind, like an itch I couldn't reach. I tried to tell myself it didn't matter.

The man at my side was Samuel. *My* Samuel. The man I once loved so fiercely. The one who I thought I'd never see again.

I should be grateful I had him back. That he let go of the anger, the darkness, the relentless need for revenge.

But the question remained, even as I did everything to convince myself this was exactly what I wanted.

Could I truly let go of Gideon Saint for good?

And what would it mean for us if I couldn't?

CHAPTER THIRTEEN

Gideon

The last rays of the setting sun painted the sky a stunning mixture of pinks and purples as I stood beside Imogene on the terrace, basking in just how normal our life had become since she was released from the hospital over a month ago.

No more revenge. No more lies. No more secrets. Just us.

It was everything we always dreamed about.

Every morning, I woke up and made her breakfast, which we ate out here as we worked on a crossword puzzle together. Afterwards, we typically went for a walk on the beach. In the afternoons, I usually spent an hour or so in our home gym while she worked with her physical therapist.

Unlike before when I would insist on spending hours sparring with Henry to build up my physical and mental endurance, now my only purpose in working out was to stay in shape.

It still felt strange not to use every free minute of my day planning the downfall of the men who betrayed me. Any time I even considered asking Henry to use his skills and track down Liam, all it took was one look at Imogene to remind me what was important. She was. Nothing else.

I had to believe that karma would eventually catch up to Liam and he would pay for what he'd done.

Maybe he already had, which would explain why his whereabouts were still unknown.

"You didn't hear a word I just said, did you?"

Imogene's voice cut through the haze of my thoughts, bringing me back to the present.

Blinking, I focused on her face, the furrow in my brow mirroring her playful look of disapproval.

"Sorry. I went somewhere else for a minute."

"Somewhere...bad?" she asked hesitantly.

I pulled her into my embrace, grateful to be able to hold her like this again without worrying about causing her pain.

"There's no more bad." I curved toward her. "Not with you in my life." She sighed into me as I lowered my mouth toward hers, savoring in the feel of her tongue briefly swiping against mine before I pulled back. "So what were you saying?"

"Just that today is the anniversary of our first kiss," she answered. "Eight years ago."

"You remember the date?"

"And the kiss. It was pretty unforgettable. I'd never been kissed like that before in my life."

"It was pretty memorable for me, too." I pulled her close as we watched the sunset together. "I almost didn't kiss you," I reminisced, recalling the turmoil I'd felt back then.

It was refreshing to finally talk about that time in my life again. To not have to hide it anymore.

"I knew if I had one taste, I'd want more. I'd want all of you."

"I had a thing for you since the second we were introduced," she confessed with a wistful look in her eyes. "I didn't think you'd be interested, considering I was still in college and you were this professional guy in your thirties."

"Oh, I was *very* interested." I playfully waggled my brows.

"What changed your mind about kissing me?"

I shifted her body to face me, keeping my arms wrapped around her waist. "I knew I'd regret it if I didn't. So when we were all spending the weekend at your uncle's lake house and I walked in on you standing in front of the refrigerator wearing just a t-shirt and a tiny pair of boy shorts, I snapped."

"I'm glad you did." She hoisted herself onto her toes, her lips brushing against mine.

"Best decision of my life." I pressed my mouth more firmly against hers, memories from that first kiss eight years ago flooding back in an instant.

Imogene threaded her fingers through my hair, igniting a fire within me as she pressed her body against mine. I couldn't get over how perfectly she fit in my arms. Like two puzzle pieces finally clicking into place after being lost for too long.

Her tongue traced the seam of my lips, and I eagerly opened for her, craving her more than I did my next breath.

These past few weeks as she healed from her injuries had been torture. I wanted nothing more than to make love to her.

But I didn't want to do anything that might hurt her, even though her bruises had faded and she no longer needed a sling.

"Please," Imogene begged, as if able to sense my inner turmoil. "I need to feel you. I don't know if I can stand waiting any longer. This may be the longest I've gone without having an orgasm and it's killing me."

I groaned, wanting more than anything to give her what she needed. "I don't want to hurt you."

"You won't. I'm better. Plus, if you don't fuck me, I'll need to break one of your rules."

"My rules?"

Biting her bottom lip, she slowly nodded. "In Pebble Beach, you forbade me from getting myself off. You said you owned all my orgasms. So are you going to get me off or do I need to take matters into my own hands?"

I stared at her for several long moments. I was about to tell her that the man who told her he owned all her orgasms wasn't me. At least I was trying not to be that man anymore. Trying to leave all traces of Gideon Saint in the past.

But one thing I learned about Imogene, as both Samuel Tate and Gideon Saint, was that it was nearly impossible to deny her.

The same remained true to this day.

"I'll always give you what you need." I gripped her hip and steered her back into the house. "Always," I repeated, about to slam my mouth against hers.

Before I could, a loud chiming ripped through the space, forcing me back to reality.

After the past few weeks of living in this bubble with Imogene, the sound of my phone ringing felt foreign and unfamiliar.

But unlike weeks ago, I ignored it. There were no

more pressing matters to discuss with Henry. My focus was on Imogene.

Nothing else.

I silenced my phone in my pocket and raked my eyes over Imogene's face. From her doe-like eyes, to her flushed complexion, to her kiss-swollen lips. She was beautiful.

And she was mine, despite everything I'd put her through. I still struggled to wrap my head around the fact that I had her. That she was so willing to forgive me. But I'd spend the rest of my life doing everything in my power to earn that forgiveness.

"I love you so damn much," I murmured as I dipped my head toward hers once more.

And yet again, my phone started ringing.

Imogene masked her annoyance with a smile, stepping out of my hold.

"Why don't you see what he wants?"

She didn't have to ask who it was. There was only one person it could be.

"If he's called twice, it must be serious."

She had a point. Not only was Henry calling after seven, which would have been after ten o'clock for him now that he was back in Atlanta, but he'd called again when I didn't answer.

He wouldn't do that if it wasn't important.

"Just give me a minute," I told her.

"Come find me when you're done. Here's a hint... I'll be the naked woman in your bed."

My dick throbbed at the image her words evoked. "You drive me crazy." I covered her mouth with mine.

"That's the point." She nibbled on my lower lip, then spun, swaying her hips as she disappeared down the hallway.

I hastily yanked my cell out of my pocket and brought it up to my ear. "What's going on?" I answered.

"Are you at Imogene's?" Henry asked, his voice somewhat panicked.

"No." I furrowed my brow. "We're at the bungalow."

"Fuck."

"What happened?" I pressed, my anxiety mounting with every second.

"The system alarmed at the back door. Do you want me to call the police?"

I stared into the distance, my brain going a mile a minute. All reason told me it was probably just someone who noticed Imogene's place had been empty, and they decided to break in.

But I couldn't ignore the unsettled feeling in my gut.

"I'll check it out."

"Are you sure?"

"You know how I feel about the police. I'd rather not involve them unless necessary."

"You'll let me know what you find?"

"Of course. Talk soon."

With that, I ended the call and shoved my phone back into my pocket.

"What's going on?"

At the sound of Imogene's voice, I darted my head up to see her lingering in the hallway, concern etched across her features.

I pushed out a sigh. "It's probably nothing, but the back door of your townhouse triggered an alarm. I need to go check it out."

"I'm coming with you." She started toward the front door.

"Absolutely not."

"You just said it's probably nothing." She crossed her arms in front of her stomach, something she wasn't able to do a few weeks ago.

"Imogene…"

"Don't Imogene me," she retorted with fire in her gaze. "You can either drive me yourself or I'll just order an Uber after you leave. Either way, I'm going. You can decide whether *you* want to drive me or let a complete stranger do the honors."

I narrowed my gaze at her, hoping she'd back down. I should have known she wouldn't.

"Fine. But you'll stay in the car until I know it's safe for you."

"I can do that." Flashing me a conniving smile, she spun around.

"Has anyone ever told you how stubborn you are?" I mumbled under my breath.

"Only you." She winked over her shoulder, then opened the door and headed outside.

CHAPTER FOURTEEN

Gideon

I parked my SUV in front of Imogene's townhouse and killed the engine, reaching into the glove box for the pistol I kept there. I turned to Imogene, her face a blend of uncertainty and determination in the dim light of the nearby streetlamp.

"Stay here. Keep the doors locked." I handed her the gun, holding her gaze. "Do you remember how to use this?"

Her expression hardened as she wrapped her fingers around the handle, keeping the barrel pointed down.

"Yes."

"Good." I started to open the door, but her voice stopped me.

"What about you?"

"I don't need a gun to defend myself, should it come to that."

"But—"

"I'll be fine. Like I said, it's probably nothing."

She forced a smile, but I sensed her reluctance to believe me.

My gut told me otherwise, too, especially now that I was here. The back of my neck tingled, a sense of premonition filling me. Which was why I wanted to make sure Imogene was armed.

"I'll be right back." With one last kiss on her forehead, I slipped out of the car and headed for the side gate that led to the back yard.

The ocean breeze was relatively calm, a strange contrast to the heavy pulse thrumming in my chest. I cautiously scanned my surroundings for anything that appeared out of place. I hadn't been here in weeks, making it difficult to discern if anything *had* been disturbed.

I climbed the short flight of stairs leading to the deck and came to a stop when I saw the back door was slightly ajar. My heart rate increased as I examined the doorjamb for any sign of forced entry, but found none. Whoever had been here had to have known Imogene's access code.

Slowly pushing the door open, I entered the townhouse with careful, measured steps. The dark silence pressed against me, amplifying every creak of the wood floors beneath my feet. I started my search in the downstairs bathroom, followed by Imogene's office, but they were undisturbed. The same was true of the living area and kitchen.

But that didn't push down my unease. Something still felt off.

On light feet, I made my way to the second floor, frowning when I noticed the door to Imogene's bedroom was shut, a glow visible through the crack between the floor and the door.

Turning the knob, I pushed the door open and the room came into view. The light from a nearby street lamp cast long shadows across the space.

But just like downstairs, it was empty, apart from her belongings. As were the ensuite bathroom and closet. Yet there was a disturbance lingering in the air. Someone had left their mark on this room. I could feel it.

Not wanting to leave Imogene alone any longer than necessary, I headed down the stairs and back outside with a nagging feeling of unease hanging over me.

"Anything?" she asked when I opened her door, her voice laced with tension.

"Nothing I could see." I took the gun from her and slipped it into the waistband of my jeans. "I want you to take a look around and see if anything stands out."

"Of course."

I helped her down from the car and guided her into

the house. Over the next several minutes, Imogene floated from room to room, checking each space with quick, assessing glances.

"Anything missing?" I asked once she'd been through each and every room. "Even if you don't notice anything, maybe something has been moved?"

She shook her head, her expression growing more perplexed by the second. "I can't really remember where I left things. The last time I was here was before the accident. I'm not..." She trailed off, her gaze landing on something in her office.

"What is it?"

She crossed the room toward the bookshelf and picked up one of the black frames containing a photo I recognized of us that was taken years ago.

Before my life was turned upside down.

"I took all the photos out of these frames. They all had photos of, well...you." Her lips curved into an apologetic smile. "Before I knew the truth, I came in here and got rid of them because I didn't think I could move on with you — Gideon — when I was still clinging to Samuel's ghost."

"Did you put them back at some point?"

She vehemently shook her head. "I put them in a box and left it over there." She pointed toward the desk before returning her attention to the bookcases. "But these... They're all exactly where I had them before I took them down. Whoever did this has been here before."

My mind raced as I tried to make sense of this.

Why would someone break in just to return old photos to her bookshelf? But as I studied them, I realized they weren't old photos. Not exactly.

"I think it's more than that," I said, blinking repeatedly as I studied each photo.

And each one only proved my theory further.

"What do you mean?" Imogene asked.

"Take a closer look." I gestured to a familiar photo of Imogene, Ollie, and me taken during one of our weekend getaways to Hilton Head.

But instead of seeing the man I used to be, the photo now contained me with my current appearance.

"How?" Imogene asked in a barely audible voice, her face wide in horror and disbelief. "Why?"

"To send a message," I gritted out through clenched teeth.

This had to be Liam's handiwork. But why go through the trouble? Why risk getting caught? It didn't make sense.

Then Imogene inhaled a sharp breath, her eyes widening as she studied another framed photo.

"What is it?"

"This one," she began, shaking her head before meeting my curious gaze. "This is recent."

"Recent?" I echoed, my heart racing as I focused on the photo.

It wasn't a picture from our past. It was taken as we walked along the beach. And not here in La Jolla, but up in Del Mar just outside our beach bungalow.

The realization hit me like a ton of bricks, and anger surged through my veins. This wasn't merely about our past.

It was about our present as well.

Yanking my phone out of my pocket, I punched Henry's contact. He picked up almost immediately.

"What did you find?" he asked.

"Liam's been here," I seethed, my voice trembling with anger.

"How do you know?"

"He left fucking photos. Doctored ones where he switched out what I used to look like with my current appearance."

"Why would he do that?"

"My guess is to fuck with me. To let me know that he knows exactly who I am. And that's not all."

"What else?"

"One of the photos is recent. Taken in Del Mar right outside of our house." My eyes flicked toward the bookshelves, my stomach churning from the invasion of privacy. The bungalow was supposed to be our sanctuary, free from shadows and darkness.

But Liam found us anyway. How?

Rage simmered inside me, and for a moment, I fantasized about all the ways I could end him, erase him from our lives for good. Make him pay for this.

"Do you want me to come back to San Diego? We can track down Liam and finish this, once and for all."

I hesitated, weighing his offer carefully. My agreement was on the tip of my tongue. The temptation to finally put an end to this was overwhelming, especially when I thought about how close he had been without either of us realizing it.

But then my gaze fell to Imogene. I promised her I'd leave my old life behind, start fresh with her. After everything she endured, she deserved that much.

"No," I finally said, my voice tight.

"Are you sure?" Henry asked, obviously surprised by my response.

I was, too.

Mere weeks ago it wouldn't have been a question of if I'd make Liam pay for this, but how.

Not anymore.

"He'll slip up eventually," I assured Henry, my words feeling hallow. "Someone will see him, and he'll get what he deserves. But not by my hand. Never again," I reiterated, unsure if it was more for his sake or mine.

CHAPTER FIFTEEN

Imogene

The darkness in the bedroom felt thick, like it might suffocate me if I let it. The shadows on the walls seemed darker than usual, the edges as sharp as a knife. I clung to Gideon's warmth as we lay in bed, listening to the soothing sounds of the ocean outside, trying to pretend I felt as safe as I once did in this place.

But even his embrace couldn't chase away the unease that had settled over me. This house now felt like just another hiding spot. A false sense of security we'd foolishly held onto, only to have our past catch up to us once again.

I shouldn't have had any trouble falling asleep. My body was physically exhausted after spending hours at my old townhouse, answering questions from the local police Gideon had called to report the break-in.

I'd gone over every detail with them until I thought my head might explode from the monotony of their questions.

Well, *almost* every detail.

I left out the fact that the man who had been in those photos was the same man he'd been replaced with.

Through it all, Gideon was a comforting presence beside me as investigators combed the house for prints and evidence, even though we both knew they wouldn't find any. Not from someone as meticulous as Liam.

I lifted my gaze toward Gideon's face, studying his features as he stared at the ceiling. The worry lines in his forehead indicated he was just as unsettled by tonight as I was. Regardless, he remained firm in his decision to let the authorities handle Liam.

It should have brought me comfort.

Instead, it made me miss the man who took out my attacker in the alley with the cold indifference of a trained killer. The man who fucked me senseless in the library of Liam's house. The man who once made me think he would burn down the world for me.

Would I ever see that man again?

I trailed my hands over his torso, mapping out the intricate pathway of scars that snaked across his skin. Each one told a story, a testament to the strength he was forced to demonstrate in order to survive what I could only describe as hell on earth.

Each one proof that the man I knew as Samuel had been irrevocably changed by what he endured.

Just like I had.

As my hand reached the angry scar marring his side where he'd been shot, he scooped it up and brought it to his lips, touching a gentle kiss to my knuckles.

"Get some sleep, Imogene. You've had a long day."

I pulled my hand from his, pressing it to his cheek and forcing his eyes to mine. "But I don't want to sleep, Gideon." I inched my lips toward his, touching my mouth to his, my tongue slipping inside.

He groaned, the sound reverberating through my body and reminding me of all the things this man made me feel. Not as Samuel, but as Gideon. The heights he was able to bring me to were unlike anything I'd ever experienced.

And right now, that was what I needed.

Not considerate, loving Samuel Tate.

But passionate, possessive Gideon Saint.

Deepening the exchange, I attempted to pull him closer, hooking a leg over his waist and slowly circling my hips.

"Imogene," he moaned, his raspy voice full of need and frustration at the same time.

"I need to feel you," I whispered breathlessly against

his mouth, trailing my hand down his chest until it slipped beneath the waistband of his pajama bottoms. "It's been too long."

He caught my wrist before I could to wrap my hand around his hardening erection, his turmoil evident in his eyes, despite the fact that he was ready to do this hours ago.

The break-in changed that.

I feared it would change everything.

"I need this. *We* need this."

With increasing determination, I moved my mouth against his again, trying to remind him of the passion and desire we once shared. Unlike before, he didn't immediately part his lips for me, his restraint and reluctance palpable.

"Please, Samuel," I murmured, using his real name for the first time in ages.

His grip on my hip hardened, his fingers digging into my skin. I could feel the heat of his body pressed against mine, but he still didn't move. He didn't retreat, either. He just held me in place, the tension between us growing with each passing second.

Finally, he exhaled a long breath and gently pushed me onto my back. When I felt his erection hit that spot I'd been dying to feel him for over a month now, I released a whimper.

"God, I love that sound." He pulled back, meeting

my eyes. "I always have. Love knowing the effect I have on you."

"Only you," I murmured, my skin prickling with heat as he ran his hand along the contours of my frame, his finger slipping under the waistband of my shorts.

His eyes flicked to mine, an unspoken question within.

But it wasn't even a question.

I needed this connection. Needed to silence the turmoil that had been plaguing me since we came home from the hospital.

Hell, since I woke up and he swore Gideon Saint was dead.

I lifted my hips, swallowing down the subtle ache from the movement.

His eyes never left mine as he slowly dragged my shorts down my legs, tossing them to the side. When I lifted my tank top over my head, his pupils flamed, his gaze focusing on my breasts.

I loved that, despite all the times he'd seen me like this, I still affected him this way. Loved that all these years later, we were still as desperate to feel each other as we were in the beginning.

His mouth covered mine in a heated kiss, his tongue swiping against mine. But despite the depth of his need, it felt...lacking. Like he was purposefully holding back.

I ran my fingers along his spine, digging my nails into

his grooved skin. He groaned into my mouth, but still kept his motions gentle.

As if scared I'd break if he pushed too hard.

"I need to taste you, Imogene. You have no idea how damn starved I've been for you."

A wave of desire surged through me, igniting a fire that had been smoldering beneath the surface for weeks now. It was exactly what I needed. The passion. The hunger. The desperation.

Meeting his eyes, I smirked. "Then what are you waiting for? Taste me." I leaned toward him, taking his earlobe between my teeth. "Make me come."

Growling, he claimed my mouth in another kiss before slowly snaking down my body, exploring and worshiping every inch of me.

When he settled between my legs and his tongue slid over my clit, I released a satisfied moan, my body melting into the mattress as weeks worth of tension rolled off me.

He slipped a finger inside me, his tongue continuing to circle me. But even when he added another finger, it still wasn't enough. It still felt like he was holding back.

"Harder," I begged, grinding my hips against him with more urgency.

"Let me enjoy this," he pressed a hand to my stomach, locking me in place. "Let me enjoy you."

Closing my eyes, I tried to lose myself in the

moment, in the sensual way he massaged my insides as his tongue traced slow circles around my clit.

But my mind drifted to that day in Liam's library. How Gideon dropped to his knees and devoured me in a way that made me certain I'd never be satisfied with another man again. How he dug his teeth into me as he fucked me. He was so unrelenting. So passionate. So damn hungry.

I missed it.

Missed *him*.

Missed the rough, dominant man who took what he wanted and didn't apologize for it.

The man who knew exactly what I needed without me having to ask.

The man who left bruises on my skin that told a story of his unrelenting need, marking me and claiming me as his.

The mere memory pushed me higher until I couldn't resist anymore, my cries echoing in the room as I unraveled.

Not because of how he made me feel now.

But because of how he once did.

Unapologetically.

Fiercely.

Completely.

"God, I love watching you come."

I opened my eyes and met his, my desire coating his

lips. Clutching his cheeks, I dragged him back up my body, not wanting him to see the truth in my gaze.

"Then get inside of me and let's see if you can make me come again."

A wicked grin crossed his face as he playfully waggled his brows. "Is that a challenge?"

"And if it is?"

"You should already know..." He shifted his weight to his hands as he placed them on either side of my head, lowering his lips to mine. "I don't like losing."

"Then let's see what you've got."

He pressed another kiss to my lips, his tongue briefly swiping with mine before he pulled back to stand. After pushing down his pants, he returned to the bed, bringing his erection up to me.

I closed my eyes, reveling in the feel of him after so long.

"Eyes on me."

The dominance and power in his voice sent a shiver down my spine. It reminded me so much of Gideon. Samuel wasn't a pushover and he definitely taught me things in the bedroom I didn't think possible. But Gideon was different. I couldn't quite explain it, considering I now knew they were the same person. But when I was with Gideon, he didn't hold anything back. He fucked me like it might be the last time he ever would.

Probably because there was a strong possibility of that being the case.

Opening my eyes, I trained them on Gideon, bracing myself for him to thrust into me, especially with the heat in his stare. Instead, he slowly pushed inside. I figured he was just letting me get acclimated to him again after nearly two months without having sex.

But even after several slow pushes, he didn't pick up his pace. He maintained his tender and steady rhythm. His lips found mine, his kiss just as gentle as the way he moved inside of me.

I let my fingers run over his back, my nails digging into his flesh as I tried to draw more from him. To find the darkness I'd fallen for.

But it wasn't there.

As incredible as he felt, it wasn't what I needed. Not right now.

I wanted to see the fierceness in his eyes. Wanted to feel his hunger consume me. Wanted a reminder of how he once made me feel more alive than anyone had in years.

Maybe ever.

"Harder." I wrapped my legs around his waist, urging him to increase his pace. "I don't want it gentle. Not tonight."

He lifted his gaze to mine, his turmoil obvious as he shook his head. "I don't want to hurt you."

I parted my lips to remind him yet again that the accident wasn't his fault, but before I could, he pressed his mouth to mine, swallowing my protest.

"Let me make love to you, Imogene. Because I am so damn in love with you."

"I love you, too," I sighed, succumbing to his affection as he moved delicately inside of me.

I squeezed my eyes shut, trying revel in the sensation of Samuel making love to me again, like I once imagined. Instead, I found myself missing the darker edges, the fierce passion Gideon exhibited in everything he did.

"Oh, Imogene," he exhaled, his rhythm increasing slightly until he stilled, jerking through his release, his lips slamming against mine.

I moaned into his mouth, savoring in the roughness of his tongue tangling with mine. But he gradually slowed his motions, the intensity of his kiss transitioning and becoming softer. Gentler. Sweeter.

Pulling back, he touched his forehead to mine, our breaths intermingling. "I love you."

I forced a smile. "I love you, too."

I *did* love him. He was my safe haven. My new beginning. My soul mate. We had a chance to be together without the shadows of his past clouding our lives.

But as he held me in his careful, measured way throughout the night, the emptiness only grew.

Weeks ago, I worried the day might come when Gideon's darkness would overtake the few pieces of Samuel that remained.

Now I couldn't help but fear that, one day soon, the last remnants of Gideon Saint would be extinguished by Samuel's light.

CHAPTER SIXTEEN

Gideon

The heat of the garage was suffocating, pressing down on me as I jabbed repeatedly at the punching bag. My fists hitting the tough leather echoed like thunder in the small space, drowning out all other sounds. The controlled burn in my muscles was the only thing grounding me right now, the only thing that kept me from letting my mind spiral. After last night, every part of me was wound tight, more like a live wire than a man who had promised to turn over a new leaf.

I truly believed I could protect Imogene by leaving all of this behind. By pretending I wasn't the monster I had no choice but to become.

Last night was a glaring reminder that I couldn't just wish my past away.

I aimed another punch at the bag, imagining Liam's face, the feeling of raw satisfaction that would come from finally erasing him from our lives pushing me faster and harder. The past few weeks had lulled me into believing I could build something good with Imogene, free of anything that had come before.

Free of my sins.

But the break-in made me realize something I'd been happy to ignore. My promise to keep Imogene safe and my determination to keep my past buried couldn't co-exist in the same world.

One of them would have to go.

The jarring chime of the doorbell broke through my thoughts, pulling me back to the present. Retrieving my cell from a nearby table, I checked the security app and found a tall, older man in a dark suit standing outside. Everything about him exuded authority — a suit too formal for the California heat, a stance too rigid to belong to anyone except someone used to waiting people out.

Grabbing a towel, I dabbed at the sweat covering my face and torso before hastily throwing a t-shirt over my head and making my way out of my makeshift gym.

"Gideon Saint?" the man asked as soon as I opened the door, his gaze cool and assessing.

I gave a slight nod. "And you are?"

"Agent Lawrence Myers. FBI." He flashed his badge before tucking it back into his suit jacket pocket. "I'd like to speak with Ms. Prescott about last night's incident." His words were measured, his eyes never leaving mine, as if searching for something.

"Agent Myers," Imogene said brightly as she appeared beside me.

With furrowed brows, I looked between Imogene and Agent Myers, her recognition making it clear they'd already met. But when?

"I'm glad to see you out of the hospital and moving around. I trust your recovery is going well?"

"It is. I'm hoping my doctor will clear me to return to work next week."

I did my best to push down my unease over the prospect, especially after last night.

"I'm sure you're looking forward to life getting back to normal."

"I certainly am. Won't you come in?"

She stepped back to allow him to enter, something I'd hoped to avoid.

As he crossed the threshold, his eyes continued to survey me. I tried to get a read on him but couldn't. Which only unnerved me even more.

"Would you like some coffee?" Imogene asked as she led him toward the living room.

"You don't have to wait on him," I admonished. "You still need to take it easy."

"I'm fine." She playfully rolled her eyes.

"No need," Myers interjected. "I won't be long."

"What can I do for you?" She gestured to the reading chair opposite her as she settled into the couch. I joined her, keeping my gaze trained on the agent.

"I just wanted to ask a few questions about the break-in last night." He reached into his pocket and retrieved a small notepad. "I must admit, I was quite surprised to learn about it from my supervisor and not from you, especially after I specifically asked you to reach out if William Pierce tried to contact you."

"With all due respect, Agent Myers," I spoke up in a firm tone. "Imogene was a bit shaken up after everything. We both were. It was nearly midnight by the time we finally finished with the local police, and all we wanted to do was go to sleep."

"That's understandable," Myers said, though there was a hint of skepticism in his voice.

Then he opened a folder and produced several images — crime scene snapshots of the framed photos left in Imogene's home.

"These were taken last night at the townhouse by the forensics team." He placed six photos on the glass coffee table between us. "Can you tell me where and when each one was taken?"

"She already told the local police everything she knew. It should be in their report," I interjected.

"I prefer to conduct my own investigation and ask

my own questions." He gritted a smile, then shifted his attention back to Imogene, arching an expectant brow.

"They were all taken years ago, except for one."

"This one?" He pointed to the more recent photo we discovered on Imogene's bookshelf.

"Yes."

"It was taken on the beach in front of this house?" Myers pressed.

Imogene nodded.

"Do you know when exactly?"

She squinted, studying the photo. "I can't be sure. It could have been any time over the past three weeks. I don't have my sling on, which I stopped wearing all the time a few weeks ago. There's nothing that stands out about our clothes to indicate a specific date. Truthfully, the days have sort of blended together lately." She returned her gaze to Agent Myers. "I'm sorry I'm not more helpful."

"Not at all." He gave her a smile that felt borderline condescending. "And the rest of the photos were taken years ago?"

She nodded once more. "Except they've been altered."

"You told the local detective that the original photos featured Samuel Tate, but in these, he's been replaced with Mr. Saint." He looked my way.

"That's correct."

"Do you know why someone would do that?"

She shook her head, parting her lips.

"Isn't it your job to figure out the motives behind a criminal's behavior?" I chimed in.

"It is. But considering you both mentioned to the local police that you suspect William Pierce is responsible for this, it seems a reasonable question given Ms. Prescott's close relationship to him." Myers returned his attention to Imogene. "Any idea why he might not only return these photos to your bookshelf after you'd taken them down, but also alter them to replace Samuel Tate's image with Mr. Saint's?"

Imogene hadn't told the investigators the truth last night. To be honest, I was actually surprised by how convincing she sounded. But there was something different about Agent Myers.

Almost like he already knew the truth.

But how?

"I can't possibly try to rationalize Liam's actions," she said finally. "I've realized I didn't know him as well as I thought I did."

"Did Mr. Pierce have access to your townhouse?" he asked, his voice smooth and controlled as he steered the conversation.

"He...he did at one point," Imogene answered. "But I changed the code a few weeks ago."

Myers arched a brow, clearly intrigued. "Can I ask why?"

She swallowed, choosing her words carefully. "My dog, Ollie...he was poisoned. Just a little over a week before the crash."

"Did you report this incident?"

Imogene's shoulders tensed, and I knew she was struggling to maintain composure. "I didn't think it was necessary. There was no proof anyone had broken in. It's possible my dog could have consumed the antifreeze when we were out for a walk, but I changed the code, just to be safe."

Myers looked back at me, and I could see the silent calculation in his eyes, as if he was trying to put a convoluted puzzle together without all the pieces.

Finally, he tucked his notepad away and pushed to stand.

"I'll let you get on with your day." He looked from me to Imogene. "If you think of anything else, make sure to call."

I escorted him to the front door, the tension in the air thickening with every step.

"I'll let you know if I find something," he stated as we stepped outside, the California sun warming my skin.

"Thank you."

He extended his hand toward me and I took it in

mine, shaking it briefly. Then he turned and started up the driveway.

But he only made it a few steps before facing me once more.

"While I'm here, do you mind if I ask you a few questions?"

"About?" I drew out, the hairs on the back of my neck standing on end.

I wasn't sure if it was because of my mistrust of law enforcement in general or because something about this guy in particular didn't sit right with me.

"The night of Ms. Prescott's attack a few months ago. It's my understanding you're a part owner of the club where it happened."

"I'm more of a silent investor. And I fail to see how that relates to last night's break-in."

"Just humor me. You came to her rescue. Did you not?"

"I did," I answered somewhat reluctantly.

"Why were you in the alley?"

"I saw a man approach Imogene in the club and her body language suggested something was off. When I noticed her follow him down the rear corridor, I trailed her into the back alley. Which is where I came across her being attacked by another man."

"Who you ended up killing."

"He had a knife to her throat and had already drawn blood. I did what I had to in order to protect her."

"And then you took Ms. Prescott to the hospital?"

"She fainted. I wanted to make sure she was okay. It was a good thing I did, since she actually had a minor concussion."

"How long did you stay?"

I wanted to tell him to call my lawyer if he hoped to continue this line of questioning, but I didn't want to do anything to make him suspicious.

"A few hours. Once Imogene was clear of the various tests they gave her and I knew she'd be okay."

"What time do you think you left?"

"I don't know. Maybe two or three in the morning. Why?"

"Are you aware that a body was found on Mr. Pierce's boat? And it belonged to the man who Imogene followed out of the club before she was attacked, Benjamin Astor?"

"I may not be well-versed in police investigations, but if a body was found on his boat, perhaps he had something to do with it."

"William Pierce has an alibi for the estimated time of death. He was with Ms. Prescott at the hospital all night, a fact corroborated by the staff there. Can you tell me where you were between the hours of three and eight in the morning after you left the hospital?"

"In bed." I maintained steady eye contact so he couldn't detect even a hint of deception.

I was glad Henry subjected me to intense interrogation techniques before I started down my path of revenge. At first, I told him it was unnecessary, but he insisted, claiming it might help me out of sticky situations.

Now I was grateful for it.

"Can anyone corroborate this?"

"Doubtful. Before I started seeing Imogene, I lived alone. I do have a security system installed at my house, complete with cameras. They'll show me arriving home. I'm happy to provide the videos for you."

I leveled a stare on him, expecting for him to end this line of questioning.

I was wrong again.

"It's my understanding you met with Alton Sinclair approximately a week before his death."

"He was interested in managing some of my assets."

"A few people claimed to have observed a heated exchange between you and Mr. Sinclair at a golf tournament in Pebble Beach a few days before his death."

I swallowed hard, doing my best to keep my breathing even. "He discovered some confidential information while at my home and used it for illegal trades."

"And yet you still hired him to manage your investments?" He scrunched his brows.

"I wasn't aware he'd snooped through my files until he accused me of planting that information. While I allowed him to handle a small percentage of my investments, I wasn't affected by his illegal activities."

"A few days after his death, you flew to Atlanta. Correct?"

"Yes."

"Around the same time James Turner was there. And Brian McGuire, a funeral director, went missing."

"I had a meeting with a startup looking for angel investors."

Again, it wasn't a complete lie. Henry had set it up so I'd have a purpose for being there, should any of my actions come to bite me in the ass later.

Like right now.

"Would you like the name and number of the group I met with?"

"That would be extremely helpful."

"I'll have my assistant send it along with the video, as well as a copy of my calendar. Now if we're done here, I'd like to check on Imogene." I glowered, as if challenging him to keep pushing me.

"My apologies for taking up so much of your time."

I nodded, then turned.

"I wouldn't blame him," he said as I was about to open the door.

I looked over my shoulder, meeting his intense gaze. "Who?"

"Samuel Tate."

I fully faced him. "Samuel Tate?"

"You're obviously familiar with who he is."

I gave a subtle nod. "He was killed several years ago."

"See, this is where my colleagues and I disagree. I like to explore every possible scenario, regardless of how unlikely it might be. And after that recording was released — the one implicating Senator Turner and Mr. McGuire in trafficking Samuel Tate for profit — it made me think. What if he's still alive?"

I pushed down the heat crawling over my cheeks, my pulse increasing.

"How?"

"I know it's a long shot, but it makes sense. Hell, if I were in his shoes and the men I knew and trusted did what these bastards did to Samuel Tate, I'd want to make them pay. I doubt I'd be able to sleep until they suffered just as I had. I'd slowly dismantle their lives until there was nothing left but ashes. Wouldn't you?"

"I'd trust karma to come for them instead of playing God myself," I answered in a firmer tone than I thought myself capable of at the moment.

Myers studied me for several excruciatingly long moments, as if trying to read my thoughts. There was something familiar about him. Not his appearance, but the way he spoke.

It rattled me more than it should have.

Finally, he stepped back and turned. "Well, you're a better man than me."

I watched as he retreated down the driveway and slid into his sedan. It wasn't until he'd driven away that I remembered to breathe.

When I'd decided to seek revenge against the men who betrayed me, I went into it knowing someone may eventually uncover the truth.

That was before Imogene. Before I realized there was something worth living for again.

That there was some*one* worth living for again.

I foolishly thought I could leave my past behind me and only look toward the future.

But with every passing day, I was starting to realize just how impossible that may be.

CHAPTER SEVENTEEN

Imogene

The waves crashing against the shore outside the bungalow used to bring me peace. But today, as I sat curled up on the couch in the living room, I could barely hear them over the thoughts racing through my mind. It probably didn't help that Gideon told me to stay inside, all things considered.

I understood his concern, but it was suffocating at the same time.

Like I was stuck in a prison.

A beautiful prison, but a prison all the same.

The only saving grace was that Melanie had driven down from LA after I told her about the photos. As comforting as her presence was, I couldn't shake the unsettled feeling consuming me. And not simply because of the break-in.

Ever since Agent Myers stopped by yesterday, Gideon had seemed even more agitated, locking himself in the gym for hours as he went to town on the punching bag. He could have just been frustrated with the fact that Liam was still out there somewhere.

I sensed it was more than that, though.

"And you're absolutely certain it was Liam?" Melanie asked in a hushed voice from beside me on the couch, curling her legs beneath her.

"The frames were left exactly where I had them before I took them down."

"Why *did* you take them down?"

I took a sip of my coffee. "Because of the memories."

"The memories?" she echoed.

I nodded. "The night I learned about Samuel's fingerprints, I felt like I was losing it."

"I remember. I walked in on you surrounded by all those newspaper and magazine clippings."

"I realized I'd never move on when I was clinging to a ghost, so I boxed up everything that reminded me of Samuel Tate...including the framed photos. I never replaced them, Mel. So whoever did this knew exactly where they were. Besides you and Gideon, Liam's the only other person who's been in my place."

"He could have paid someone to do it."

"I'm not sure that's any better," I replied honestly. "At least if it's Liam, I know who to look out for. If he's paying someone to do this?" I pulled my hoodie closer to my body, goosebumps prickling my skin at the mere thought. "I just want him found so we can move on with our lives."

"And Sam...Gideon...whoever he is..." She waved her hand around, her uncertainty about what to call him obvious. "He has no desire to...you know?" She gave me a pointed look.

"He says he wants to leave Gideon Saint in the past. Technically, he still needs to use that name, but that's the only thing remaining of who he's been this past year."

She brought her mug up to her lips and took a sip of coffee, her brows furrowed in contemplation.

"How do you feel about that?"

I stared into the distance, trying to make sense of the warring thoughts in my head. "I should be thrilled he's ready to move on from all that."

"But *are* you?"

"I'll always love Samuel Tate."

"But you miss Gideon Saint," she finished. "Don't you?"

I exhaled a long breath, grateful to have her here to give me someone to talk to about everything. This had been consuming my thoughts more and more, especially after I tried to get him to fuck me the other night and he insisted on going slow.

"He treats me like I'm glass. Like he's afraid of breaking me."

"He's probably still carrying a bunch of guilt over the accident. You should have seen him at the hospital, Ginny. I'd never seen him so distraught before."

"I know. It's just... He's different now. Too...gentle."

She tilted her head. "Like, during sex?"

I nodded. "It's still good, but it's not the same. He used to be so hungry. Now there's less passion and fire. I guess that's what I'm struggling with. I miss the intense need Gideon always had for me."

"Have you talked to him about this? In my experience, keeping an open line of communication in the bedroom is important."

I bit my lower lip. "Not yet. The other night was the first time we had sex since the accident. And even then, it was only because I begged him to finally sleep with me."

"I see."

"He said all the right things. Had all the right moves. But it still felt...lacking. When he was still Gideon Saint, there was this undeniable spark between us. This thrilling sense of mystery and danger that excited me. He exuded power and control. Now, it's like he's deliberately suppressing all of that. Like he's trying to be everything Gideon wasn't. Even Samuel had more passion than this man he's become."

Melanie reached over, placing a comforting hand on mine. "You need to give it time, Ginny. You two have been through more than most people can even fathom. Now you're figuring out who you are. Figuring out what your relationship will look like, given everything that's happened. You can't expect things to be all unicorns and rainbows right away. You both have a lot to work through. But if there's anyone who can do it, it's the two of you." She paused, her eyes surveying me before remarking, "Maybe you need to get away from here."

"What? Like a vacation?"

"You've been cleared to travel, right?"

I nodded.

"Then maybe this is what you need. What you *both* need. Time away to remember what it's like to be together without the weight of the past hovering over you. Just the two of you, without distractions. You both deserve that."

The thought sent a glimmer of possibility through me. I couldn't deny that I liked the idea of getting away. Going somewhere without ghosts, without the memories and threats that seemed to linger no matter how much I wanted to escape them.

"Maybe you're right."

"Haven't you realized by now?" she replied with a smirk.

"What's that?"

"I'm *always* right."

CHAPTER EIGHTEEN

Imogene

The sound of footsteps cut through the peacefulness surrounding me as I sat in a reading chair beside the floor-to-ceiling windows in the living room, relishing in the last few moments of daylight. My heart skyrocketed into my throat and I briefly worried it was Liam. It was a baseless concern, considering all the security in place around the bungalow. After the past few days, though, I couldn't help but let my fears get the better of me.

Seconds later, Gideon strolled into the kitchen, his eyes distant, lost in thought. He was dressed in shorts and a hoodie, having spent the better part of the afternoon working out in the garage. As usual.

The late afternoon light cast shadows across his face,

making him look sharper. Colder. As if some part of him had been carved away, leaving only his rough edges.

He opened one of the cabinets and retrieved a bottle of scotch, pouring several fingers and taking a long gulp. He set the glass on the counter, staring at it for a moment before he finally looked up and noticed me studying him.

"What are you doing?" he asked, his voice flat.

"Enjoying the sunset. Or as much of the sunset I *can* from in here."

He took another long sip from his drink, then made his way toward me, lowering himself into the chair beside mine and focusing his gaze on the horizon.

After several silent moments, his eyes shifted from the window, floating over me like he was assessing me for damage.

"How's Melanie?"

"She's good. Just worried."

His jaw tightened, but he said nothing. Simply turned his gaze back toward the horizon, the sky darkening with every second.

Lately, every glance, every word seemed like a version of someone I barely recognized. This man in front of me wasn't Gideon Saint. But he wasn't Samuel Tate, either. The space between us felt wider than ever, a divide that threatened to swallow us whole.

"Why don't we get away?" I suggested after several

more moments, unsure how much longer I could stand this tension between us.

While I hated Liam for breaking into my house and destroying all sense of security, I hated him even more for this. For creating this unbearable rift between Gideon and me.

"Get...away?"

"Exactly. Let's get out of this place for a few days. Go somewhere without all of this hanging over us." I linked my fingers with his, savoring in the feel of his skin on mine.

His expression softened, the turmoil and frustration that had been plaguing him momentarily disappearing.

"We could go to Hilton Head like we used to. We can go to that hole in the wall restaurant where we both ate all those oysters and clams. Get drunk on cheap beer. Forget about life for a minute."

"That sounds amazing," he sighed, a smile teasing his lips. It was the first genuine smile I'd seen since the break-in. But in mere seconds, his expression fell and he pulled away from me, standing. "I don't think it's a good idea."

I blinked repeatedly, feeling like the rug had just been pulled out from underneath me.

"Why not?" I shot to my feet.

"Because it's not safe." His voice was calm, but there was a hardness there, making it clear this wasn't up for discussion. "I can keep you safe here. In these four walls. The security is state-of-the art. There are cameras and sensors. I know that no harm will come to you here. But anywhere else?" He shook his head. "I can't risk it."

"So...what?" I bit out, my frustration bubbling up. "Are you just going to keep me locked up here forever?"

He reached for my hand in an attempt to soothe me. "I'm just trying to protect you."

I ripped my hand from his. "Protect me?" The words came out sharper than I'd intended, but I didn't stop. "You're treating me like I'm made of glass. Like I might break. Hell, you won't even fuck me like you used to when you were—"

I stopped short, inhaling a sharp breath.

"When I was...what?"

I hesitated, my words stuck in my throat. I hadn't expected to have this conversation with him when I proposed going away on a romantic weekend together.

I could have dropped it. Hell, that was probably what I should have done. But I couldn't deny how much I missed the dark parts of him.

"When you were Gideon," I finally confessed. "When you were wild and rough and hungry." I stepped toward him, closing the gap between us until there was barely a breath separating us. "When you touched me without hesitation. Without treating me like you're worried I might break."

"Imogene," he begged, his jaw tense, as if struggling to reconcile the two parts of himself.

"I love you," I continued, placing my hand on his cheek. "I will *always* love Samuel Tate. But I miss Gideon Saint. I miss his hunger and passion. Miss the darkness that matched my own." I hoisted myself onto my toes, my lips hovering near his. "I miss how alive he made me feel."

His Adam's apple bobbed up and down in a hard swallow as his gaze traced over my face. From my eyes. To my nose. Then settling on my lips. He cupped my cheek, his touch gentle at first before becoming harsh. Powerful. Controlling.

A shadow crossed over his eyes, the heat I'd missed since the accident slowly returning.

But it disappeared in a heartbeat, and he quickly dropped his hold on me, as if reminding himself who he was.

Or, more accurately, who he *wanted* to be.

"I told you. Gideon Saint is dead." He spun from me, storming toward the front door.

But I wasn't going to let him avoid this conversation. Wasn't going to let him keep pretending to be someone I knew in my heart he wasn't.

"He's not dead." I grabbed his hand, forcing him to come to an abrupt stop. "He's still a huge part of you."

I swallowed down the emotions bubbling up inside

of me. But I couldn't stop. Not now that I was finally giving voice to all my thoughts and feelings.

"I get that the accident...changed you."

"I could have lost you, Imogene." He swallowed hard, his eyes filled with the panic he must have experienced that day. "And it would have been all my fault. I—"

"But you didn't lose me. I'm still here. I don't want you to pretend to be someone you're not because you think that's what I need. You can't pretend the past didn't happen. Can't pretend all those horrible things never happened. They did. I hate that they did, but it made you into the man you are today." I erased the distance between us once more, holding his face in my firm grip to prevent him from escaping this. "I love that man. Love his light. Love his heart. And I love his darkness, too. Please... Let me love that darkness."

He gripped my hip, his fingers digging into the skin. It ached, but I welcomed the pain. Welcomed the hurt. It was what I needed.

"Please," I said again, his blue eyes swirling with confusion and indecision. "Give me your darkness."

Closing my eyes, I inched my lips toward his, bracing for him to capture my mouth in a heated kiss like he once did.

Instead, he released me, practically pushing me away.

"I am not that person anymore," he said, his tone harsh, his expression strained with the anger he struggled to hide. "If you don't want to be with me like this, then I guess you don't want to be with me at all."

His words caught me off guard, and I stared at him, bewildered, struggling to come up with something to say. Something to make him see what I did.

But before I could, he stormed out of the house, slamming the door behind him with a finality I hadn't anticipated.

CHAPTER NINETEEN

Gideon

My tires squealed as I peeled out of the driveway of the bungalow and sped down the tranquil street. With no destination in mind, I drove aimlessly at first, my mind a jumbled mess of frustration and confusion. How could Imogene say that? How could she *want* that?

After everything I'd done, everything I'd become as Gideon Saint, how could she possibly miss him?

I thought she'd be glad to have Samuel back, the man who once dreamed of simple, beautiful things, like building a life with her. Having a family together. Being one of those couples who was still madly in love, even when we were old and gray. I was trying to give her that, trying to be that man again.

I thought it was what she wanted. What she deserved.

Wasn't it?

After driving around for a while, I pulled into the parking lot of a dive bar on the edge of town. It wasn't normally the type of place I'd frequent, but tonight it was what I needed. A place where I could disappear for a while. Where nobody gave a shit about who I was or what I'd done.

I made my way into the dimly lit room, passing a few other patrons scattered at tables or hunched over the counter. Sliding onto a worn barstool, I ordered a whiskey. The bartender didn't ask questions, just poured and left me to my thoughts. I downed half the glass on the first swallow, but the burn did nothing to dull the ache in my chest.

What did Imogene want from me? Did she want me to lose myself in that darkness again? To become the man who'd stop at nothing to settle a score? I couldn't do that, not for her. Not for anyone. That man nearly killed her.

A faint buzzing in my pocket pulled me out of my spiraling thoughts. I fished out my phone, expecting to see Imogene's name.

Instead, Henry's name flashed on the screen.

"What did you find?" I answered gruffly, trying to hide my disappointment.

"Nice to hear your voice too, buddy," Henry dead-panned, his tone light but laced with curiosity. "You okay?"

"I'm fine," I lied. "What did you find on Myers?"

After the agent's surprise visit yesterday, I'd been on edge. Something about him didn't sit right with me, especially once I learned he'd paid Imogene a visit in the hospital. I couldn't help but find it incredibly suspicious that he just so happened to stop by during one of the few times I wasn't around. It was almost like he'd purposefully waited to get her alone.

I wanted to know why.

"Your boy's squeaky clean," Henry answered. "Exemplary FBI record, not a single black mark. Same for his teaching."

"Teaching?"

"He teaches criminology and profiling classes at various colleges in the area. The staff and students all love him. In fact, his classes usually have a long waitlist."

"What about his personal life?" I pressed, taking another long sip of my drink, growing more irritated with every passing second.

"Same story there. He's spotless. Pays off his credit card in full every month. Goes to church every Sunday, although we both know that doesn't necessarily mean shit."

"You're right about that," I huffed, recalling the horror we endured at that foster home from two people who purported to be righteous and Godly.

They were anything but.

"He coaches his niece's swim team," he continued. "Volunteers at a local soup kitchen. He even donates to charities for families of fallen officers. Real choir boy stuff."

I pushed out a long breath, my shoulders falling. "So he's legit."

I'd really hoped he might find something to corroborate the feeling in my gut.

"That's one way to look at it," Henry offered. "But no one's this clean without a reason. Either he's hoping to be the next Captain America, or he's hiding skeletons so deep even the Bureau doesn't know about them."

"Think you can find out which one it is?"

Henry laughed. "I can find out anything, but it'll take some time. I'll let you know what I dig up."

"Thanks, brother."

"Any time." There was a pause, then Henry cleared his throat, his tone losing its typical banter. "How's Imogene doing, all things considered?"

"Fine," I bit out as I swallowed down another gulp of whiskey, finishing off the glass. The bartender lifted the bottle, and I nodded. He moved toward me, refilling my glass with more amber liquid.

"That tells me she's not fine. Or, more accurately, you're not. What's going on?"

I sighed, running a hand over my face. "We got into it tonight."

"What happened?"

"She suggested we get away for a while. Maybe go to Hilton Head of all places. Said we needed time to reconnect. I told her it wasn't safe, and things just escalated from there." I hesitated for a beat before confessing, "She said she misses him."

"Who? Liam?"

"Of course not," I retorted quickly, glancing over my shoulder to make sure no one was eavesdropping. Then I whispered, "Gideon Saint."

"Oh."

"How could she say that? How could she even feel that way after everything?" I lowered my voice. "She almost died because of him... Me. Because of the things I've done. I thought..." I trailed off, struggling to get my thoughts in order. "I thought she'd be happy with my decision to walk away from that life. From that person. Thought she'd be happy to have Samuel back."

"But does she?"

I furrowed my brow. "What do you mean?"

"Does she really have Samuel back?"

"Of course she does. I walked away from my plan. Even after the break-in, I haven't asked you to put your skills to use and track down Liam so I could end him, even if I've fantasized about it."

"That may be true, but that doesn't mean you're the same person you were all those years ago."

"But—"

"She's not the same person, either," he continued before I could finish my thought. "You've both changed. You've both been through some pretty horrible shit, especially you. You can't just expect to bury that part of yourself and pretend it never existed. You can't expect her to, either."

I parted my lips to argue once more, and again he interjected before I could.

"I get it, man. You're trying to do the right thing. But you can't just act like the past never happened. It's part of you, whether you like it or not."

"I don't want to be that man anymore," I said, my voice tight. "Imogene deserves better than that."

"But it sounds like Imogene doesn't want that. She doesn't want just Samuel or just Gideon. She wants all of you. She *loves* all of you. The good, the bad, the messy. That's what love is. Remember how you felt when you learned Turner hit her? When you saw her being wheeled into the hospital on that stretcher? When you didn't know if she'd wake up?"

I swallowed hard, not wanting to go back to that

night. I'd done everything in my power to forget about it. To move on from my biggest regret.

"Remember that feeling. Because if you keep trying to cut off parts of yourself to fit into some mold of what you think she deserves, you *will* lose her. After everything you've been through, is that *really* what you want?"

CHAPTER TWENTY

Imogene

The comforting aroma of sugar and vanilla enveloped me as I rolled out the dough for yet another batch of cookies. The countertops were a mess. Flour dusted every surface, bowls and measuring spoons scattered everywhere. A tower of cookies sat cooling on a rack, alongside a tray of cupcakes waiting to be frosted.

Baking had always been my solace, a way to calm my nerves and find peace in the midst of chaos or uncertainty.

Not tonight.

After my argument with Gideon, nothing could calm me. I kept replaying it over in my head. Each time, his words cut deeper than before.

Was I wrong to tell him how I felt? To want him to be someone he might not be anymore?

But I didn't think that was the case. If anything, it felt like he was trying to be someone he wasn't. I didn't want him to pretend anymore. I wanted him to be free to be who he was, even if that man had a dangerous streak.

The front door creaked open, cutting through the stillness. I glanced at the clock on the stove to see it was nearly two in the morning. Gideon had been gone for hours, and I hadn't heard his car pull into the driveway.

I froze, the cookie cutter poised mid-air, my heart slamming against my ribs as I strained to listen. Then I heard footsteps, faint but unmistakable.

It couldn't be Gideon. He never moved like that — slow, methodical. His steps were always brisk and purposeful.

I scanned the room, frantically searching for something I could use to defend myself. My eyes landed on a rolling pin sitting on the edge of the counter. Not an ideal weapon, but it was better than nothing.

The footsteps grew closer, and I snatched the rolling pin, gripping it as tight as I could. The air seemed to thicken, the hum of the oven fading beneath the pounding of my pulse.

I positioned myself just around the corner, ready to strike at whoever emerged from the hallway.

Another step. Then another. Then a shadow stretched into view. My grip tightened on the rolling pin and I held my breath.

Then the stranger stepped into the light.

But it wasn't a stranger after all.

"Imogene?"

The air whooshed out of my lungs in a relieved gasp at Gideon's familiar voice. My arms dropped to my sides, the rolling pin slipping from my fingers and hitting the floor with a clatter.

"What are you doing?" His brow furrowed as he took in the scene.

"I thought...," I stammered, adrenaline still coursing through my veins. "I don't know. I guess I assumed you were sleeping at the other house tonight since it's so late. When I heard the door open, I thought—"

"Someone was breaking in."

"I know it's essentially impossible, but still..."

"I'm sorry." He stepped toward me, but didn't attempt to comfort me. "I didn't mean to scare you." His gaze floated over me, then the rolling pin, and finally the chaos of the kitchen. "Baking." He laughed under his breath. "It always did relax you when you were stressed."

"Usually." I turned from him, refocusing my attention on cutting out sugar cookies.

"But not tonight?"

There was a hint of something in his voice. Sadness? An apology maybe?

"Not tonight."

I pressed the cookie cutter into the dough, then glanced over my shoulder. I was about to ask him what he was doing back here, but stopped when I spied the suitcase off to the side. I hadn't noticed it when he first walked in. Now it seemed to have an unavoidable presence.

"Going somewhere?" I asked, trying to sound casual, but my voice cracked.

Did he only come back so he could pack up his things?

"Yes. At least I hope so."

I crossed my arms in front of my chest. "You hope so?"

He shrugged, the confident man he typically was nowhere to be found. "That all depends on you."

"Me?"

"I've been trying so damn hard to be the man you deserve. When I saw them wheel you into the hospital after that accident..." He shook his head, his expression strained. "I figured it was the least I could do."

"But I don't want you to be the man you *think* I deserve," I exclaimed, my frustration over the situation increasing yet again.

It felt like we were just replaying a broken record over and over again. But if this was what I needed to do in order for him to finally understand, I would.

"I want you to be the man you already are. Because I'm in love with that man. Even the dark, damaged parts. In fact, I think I love those parts even more. I don't want this ideal of perfection you've somehow convinced yourself I deserve. I want real."

He stared at me for what felt like an eternity. I expected for him to reiterate his argument against being that man. To my surprise, he stepped closer, touching his thumb and forefinger to my chin, forcing my eyes toward his.

It wasn't a firm grip, but there was still something powerful about it.

"What did you miss?" he asked, his tone full of something I hadn't heard in too long now.

"What do you mean?" I whimpered.

"What parts of Gideon Saint have you missed?"

I swallowed hard, my pulse increasing as desire flooded my veins.

"The way he looked at me with so much heat that I thought I'd combust."

His pupils flamed as his greedy gaze raked over every inch of my frame, causing a shiver to roll through me. It reminded me of my birthday party. How, even when

Liam paraded me around, I still felt Gideon's eyes on me. Still felt the heat of his stare. Still felt his hunger.

"Like that?" he asked, pulling my body into his.

"Y-yes," I stammered, my mouth growing dry.

He curved toward me, nuzzling the crook of his neck. "What else, Imogene?"

It was a good thing he was holding me. Otherwise I wouldn't be surprised if I melted into a puddle on the floor. It had been so long since I felt anything remotely close to this, and I didn't want this moment to end.

"The way your beard scraped at my skin. Then how you'd bite me, marking me and letting everyone know I was yours."

Without a single ounce of hesitation, he wrapped a hand around my hair, forcing my head to the side. Then he clamped his teeth on my neck, rough and unforgiving.

The ache was almost unbearable. Not because it hurt, although there was certainly a bit of pain. But because of how much I needed him, especially now that he was no longer pretending to be someone he wasn't.

"Like that?" he panted, his breathing growing ragged.

As was mine.

"Yes," I replied again, my core clenching with need.

"What else, Imogene?" he pressed once more, running his finger over the place he just marked me, his tenderness a striking contrast from the way he currently looked at me. "What else did you miss about Gideon Saint?"

I drew in a deep breath in an attempt to calm the nerves fluttering in my stomach. Then I leveled him with a determined stare, hoping to sound more confident than I felt.

"The way he fucked me. How he always gave me exactly what I needed. Even if I didn't quite realize what that was."

He trailed his fingers along my collarbone, his eyes softening as he tenderly caressed my skin. A part of me worried I overstepped.

It wasn't that the sex had ever been bad between us, even as Samuel. But with Gideon, it was always so much more.

He was uninhibited. Unbridled. Unrestrained. It was why I craved it.

Outside of the bedroom, he was always so controlled. So disciplined. So...guarded.

But during those moments of intimacy when it was just us, he could let loose. He could stop allowing the weight of his past to burden him. He could be...free.

"I promise you, Imogene." He lowered his lips to mine, the warmth of his breath so close to my mouth unhinging me. "From this moment forward, I will always give you exactly what you need." He moved his hand to my throat, loosely wrapping his fingers around it.

"Always," he repeated as he tightened his grip, his mouth capturing mine in a kiss I felt everywhere.

His tongue slid against mine, resolute and determined. There was nothing hesitant or apprehensive about it. Not like the other night. Instead, the way he held me, the way he kissed me left absolutely no question in my mind exactly what this man wanted. Who he was.

He guided me out of the kitchen, his lips never leaving mine, his kiss consuming me. It had been too long since he kissed me like this. With so much passion. So much greed. Like he didn't care if he broke me. In fact, I *wanted* him to break me. Wanted him to completely shatter me into millions of pieces.

"You know I love you more than anything, right?" he asked when we reached the bedroom.

I may have had my doubts about a lot of things in my life, but this man's devotion to me was never one of them. Even when I didn't know who he was, I knew he cared deeply for me.

"Of course."

"Good." He pressed his lips against mine in another kiss that left me desperate for more. "Because tonight, I'm going to do things to you that may make you think otherwise."

A shiver rolled down my spine at what that may entail. Then he narrowed his stare on me.

But that wasn't the right word for the way he looked

at me. This was so much more than a stare. It was a reawakening. A resurrection. A rebirth.

"Strip."

His command left no room to argue. And I had no intention of arguing. Not now that I had this part of him back.

With my eyes trained on his, I lifted my shirt over my head before reaching behind me to unclasp my bra. Then I linked my fingers into the waistband of my shorts and pushed them down my legs along with my panties, kicking them to the side.

As much as he wanted to play it calm and cool, I could see how much the sight of me affected him. It didn't matter how many times he'd seen me naked. The hunger in his stare made me feel like it was our first time.

He looped his arm around me and pulled me against him. "You're so fucking beautiful."

"So are you."

His mouth covered mine, his tongue dipping inside and caressing mine, his hands roaming my frame. But it wasn't enough. Now that the emotional distance had disappeared, I didn't want anything between us.

Tearing out of the kiss, I reached for his hoodie. "Your turn."

Electricity crackled in the air between us, neither one of us saying a word as I slowly lowered the zipper, revealing more and more of him. More of the man I loved with every fiber of my being.

Once the zipper was undone, I pushed the fabric down his arms.

But as I raked my gaze over his torso, I inhaled a sharp breath and flung my eyes toward his, only to be met with a sinful smile.

CHAPTER TWENTY-ONE

Gideon

Imogene blinked repeatedly as she floated her stare between my torso and my face, clearly taken aback by what she'd discovered.

Hours ago, the skin was unblemished, apart from my scars.

Now, black ink covered the angry mark where Brian McGuire patched me up after removing the bullet, the symbol of unconditional love in the same place as the one on Imogene's body.

"I don't..." She shook her head. "When did you do that?"

"Tonight." I laughed under my breath. "It's why I was so late getting home. I wanted to do something to prove I'm finally done pretending to be someone I'm not."

"By getting a tattoo?"

"Exactly." I cupped her face, needing to see her eyes. "I've let my past dictate my life since I escaped. Wore these scars like a badge of honor. I didn't realize the control I'd allowed them to have over me. I refuse to give them that power anymore. Refuse to pretend to be someone else anymore."

She peered at me for several long moments. Then she flung her arms around me, pressing her mouth firmly against mine. As I lost myself in her kiss, it felt like a huge weight had finally been lifted off my shoulders.

She moved from my lips, trailing kisses along my jawline and down my neck, kissing each and every scar as she slowly made her way down my body.

When she lowered herself to her knees, my pupils flamed, jaw ticking. But instead of ridding me of my shorts, she focused her attention on the new mark on my skin, torturing me even more.

With gentle fingers, she traced the familiar design over the clear bandage protecting it. But as she admired it, a small furrow creased her brow. Now that she saw it up close, she realized it wasn't an exact replica of her tattoo. Instead, woven into the symbol was her name.

"You're it for me," I exhaled, touching my hand to her cheek.

Her eyes met mine. "And you're it for me, Gideon." She pressed her lips to the tattoo, her touch light and sensual. "Samuel." She dragged her tongue along the waistband of my shorts, causing a groan to vibrate in my throat.

Looking up at me with her doe eyes, she pushed my shorts down my legs and my cock sprang free, already throbbing with a desperate need to bury myself deep inside her. To finally let loose and succumb to the urges I'd tried to lock away in order to be the man I thought she deserved.

"Imogene," I growled when she wrapped her hand around my erection, sliding it up and down in a slow rhythm. Every stroke was fucking torture.

After the restraint I forced myself to exhibit over the past several weeks, I didn't want it slow or gentle. I knew she didn't either.

Grabbing her head in my hands, I dug my fingers into her hair, my grip tight.

"Open."

One word. Two syllables. Four letters.

But by her response, you'd think I just whispered my most lewd and offensive thoughts. It left no question in my mind how much she loved when I was like this. When I told her what to do. When I took complete control of her.

With her gaze locked on mine, she moistened her lips

with her tongue. I tightened my grip on her head even more, the anticipation of that tongue being on my dick driving me fucking crazy. Then she opened her mouth, eagerly awaiting my next order.

"Good girl," I praised in a low, husky voice. "Now taste."

She didn't say anything in response. Instead, she did as I requested, bringing her mouth up to my erection. As she ran her tongue along the tip, tasting the bit of pre-cum, I released a hiss, my fingers digging even harder into her scalp. I needed to hold on as tightly as I could in order to keep myself grounded when I felt like I was ready to lose my damn mind. Especially when she teased my length with her tongue before taking me completely in her mouth.

She attempted to move, but she couldn't, my hold on her too firm. My god, she looked fucking beautiful on her knees with my dick in her mouth, her expectant eyes locked on mine.

"Do you want it?" I ground out.

She managed a subtle nod.

"Good. You know what to do if it becomes too much. Three taps on my arm."

She nodded again.

"Show me," I told her, as I always did before doing this.

Blinking, she gave my forearm three taps.

"Good."

Holding her head in place, I started moving in and out of her, slowly at first, savoring the sensation of her lips wrapped around me. But within seconds, I picked up the pace, leaving her completely at my mercy. Using her for my own pleasure.

And when a moan fell from her throat, I knew she loved everything about it. That she wanted even more.

"Relax your jaw, baby," I grunted as I continued thrusting into her, making her eyes water. "Let me in."

She blinked, relaxing her jaw. When I drove in again, I hit the back of her throat, the sensation almost too much, especially when I noticed her struggle to breathe. But she still didn't look away. Still didn't tap out.

"Touch yourself," I demanded, my own breathing growing ragged.

Without hesitation, she leaned back on her heels and spread her legs, bringing her finger to her clit and rubbing.

"You can do better than that," I panted. "Fuck your cunt while I fuck your face."

She whimpered, but like the good girl she was, she followed my instructions, inserting a finger, then another, the sound of her slickness echoing in the room.

"That's it. Let me hear how wet you are. How turned on you are with a mouthful of my cock."

She moaned again, the sound intermingling with my

ragged breaths. I didn't know how much longer I'd last, but I'd be damned if I got off before she did.

"Faster," I demanded, and she thrust her fingers in and out of her pussy with more intensity. I increased my rhythm, too, pushing into her mouth with a wild urgency, continually hitting the back of her throat.

Then I drove into her one final time, keeping her head locked in place as I buried myself deep in her throat.

She darted her wide eyes to mine, obviously having trouble breathing.

"Keep going, Imogene. Don't stop. Let me hear that slick cunt."

She obeyed, plunging her fingers in and out of herself faster and faster, the lack of oxygen propelling her higher and higher. I kept my eyes trained on her, ready to pull out if I felt it was too much. Finally, her body climaxed, the vibration of her whimpers against my cock nearly setting me off, too.

I quickly pulled out and yanked her to her feet, crashing my lips to hers. Covering her heart with my hand, I breathed into her like I always did. Our kiss was desperate and hungry as we both used the opportunity to get our labored breathing under control.

Once I felt her pulse slow, I finally pulled away, grabbing her hand in mine. With my eyes locked with hers, I brought it to my mouth, sucking on the two fingers she just used to get herself off.

"Fucking delicious."

She moaned as I swirled my tongue along her fingers. Then I stepped back, hardening my expression once more.

"Get on the bed. Hands and knees. Face forward."

She instantly did as I asked, willingly obeying my command.

I didn't approach her right away, even though the mere sight of her like this made me want to explode, especially when I noticed how slick with desire her thighs were. Instead, I took a moment to appreciate how beautiful she was. How perfect she was.

How *mine* she was.

After several long moments, she glanced over her shoulder. "What are you—"

"I told you. Face forward. Unless you want to be punished."

She snapped her gaze forward once more. But I could see the effect my words had on her, a shiver rolling through her body.

My steps echoed in the room as I moved closer before crawling on the bed behind her.

"You like that, don't you?" I curved toward her, biting her neck as I ran my hand up her leg. "Like the idea of being punished."

She squeezed her eyes shut, remaining silent. I shouldn't have been surprised. I knew how much she struggled to give voice to her darker desires. I wanted her to be free with me. She was willing to accept the darkest parts of my soul. And I was more than happy to cater to the darker parts of hers.

"It's okay," I murmured. "Don't fight it. Don't pretend to be someone you're not."

"Y-yes."

"Yes...what?"

"I like the idea of being punished."

I moved my hand down her thigh, slipping it between her trembling legs and pinching her clit. As I did, she moved against me. I immediately stopped, landing a hard smack to her ass.

She yelped, but based on how wet she was, I could tell she enjoyed it.

"You want me to spank you?" I leaned closer again, rubbing my hand along her ass. "Do you think that's an appropriate punishment for failing to follow orders?"

"Yes," she moaned, grinding against me, desperate for my touch.

"Good girl." I nibbled on her neck once more. "But that leads to another question... Do I spank your ass?"

Straightening, I reeled back and landed a blow to her ass, eliciting another yelp, which turned into a moan when I caressed the reddened skin.

"Or your pussy?"

She sucked in a breath, but didn't do anything to put an end to our game. Instead, she spread her legs even more, inviting me to do as I pleased.

I licked my lips, praying I'd last long enough to get through this when my cock was practically begging for me to finally thrust into her. Then I landed a soft slap against her pussy. She didn't even flinch or show any sign of discomfort. Instead, she rocked into the sensation, burying her face in the pillow as if overwhelmed.

"Mmm...," I crooned, leaning over her and taking her earlobe between my teeth. "Seems you enjoy that one even more. And like I just promised... I'll always give you exactly what you need."

Leaving her with one last nibble on her neck, I straightened again, lightly hitting her pussy with my hand, starting her out easy. But as my own desperation to get off increased, so did my rhythm and intensity. Her moans mixed with yelps and groans until she couldn't control it anymore, her screams filling the room as another orgasm ripped through her.

I didn't give her a chance to come down. I couldn't.

I grabbed her hips and thrust into her, relief consuming me from the feel of her still clenching walls around me. I didn't take it slow. Instead, I went after her like a man obsessed. And that was exactly what I was. I was utterly obsessed with this woman. With the way she made me feel.

With the way she accepted me, regardless of my faults.

Or maybe she accepted me *because* of my faults.

I hated that it took me this long to finally realize this.

I tried to hold on, tried to prolong it, but it had been so long since I allowed myself to give in to my needs like this. Before I could stop it, I spilled into her, my body jerking and spasming through my release. I moved my hands down her arms, linking my fingers with hers as I struggled to come down from the high only this woman could give me.

Gradually slowing my movements, I showered kisses all over her skin.

"I love you."

"And I love you." She looked over her shoulder at me. "Samuel. Gideon. And all the pieces of you."

I pressed a soft kiss to her mouth, our tongues briefly tangling.

Carefully pulling out of her, I helped her onto her back and wrapped her in my arms, basking in the unwavering devotion she had for me.

Since the accident, I tried to bury Gideon Saint. I thought that was the only way I could do right by her.

It took almost losing her again for me to admit the truth.

Gideon Saint was a part of me. As was Samuel Tate.

Instead of pretending to be someone I wasn't, it was time for me to embrace all parts of myself — the good *and* the bad.

The dark *and* the light.

Just as Imogene had.

CHAPTER TWENTY-TWO

Imogene

The sunlight was soft as it spilled into the bedroom, painting the walls in hues of gold and amber. I lay beside Gideon, my head nestled against his shoulder, finding comfort in the steady rise and fall of his chest beneath me. A smile tugged at my lips as I reflected on the events of last night, marveling at how different things were now that we finally shared our truths.

I absentmindedly ran my fingers over his new tattoo that covered the old bullet wound, my name intricately woven into the swirling pattern. I wasn't sure why the tattoo surprised me so much. But it gave me hope we'd make it through this and have the happily ever after we both deserved.

Moving from the tattoo, I continued my exploration

of his body, tracing the various scars. Each one told a story. A map of his pain. A testament to how much he endured in order to survive.

"That one," he began in a low, rough voice as I brushed my fingers along the jagged line near his ribcage, "is from a knife."

I stilled, looking up at him, surprised by his words.

For weeks, he purposefully avoided talking about anything remotely relating to that time of his life. As if it would make it disappear from his past.

Not anymore.

And I wanted to know everything he suffered, regardless of how painful it might be to hear.

"Sometimes we got to choose our weapons," he explained, his words devoid of emotion, like he was reciting someone else's story. "Other times, they were chosen for us. This was one of the times they chose for us. Of course, they didn't tell me my opponent used to be a butcher. He knew exactly how to cut a man without killing him, at least not right away. Every slice was calculated, meant to weaken me, bleed me out just enough to give him the upper hand. To really put on a good show. After all, if you put on a good show, the powers-that-be might fix a fight to make sure you won. Make sure you kept winning."

My heart clenched, tears stinging my eyes as I fought to keep my emotions in check. He didn't need my pity.

He'd made that clear before. But how could I not ache for what he'd endured? How could I not want to take that pain and carry it for him?

"I got lucky," he said. "He got too confident, and I managed to disarm him." He let out a humorless chuckle. "But luck only gets you so far in a place like that."

I looked up at him, my eyes tracing over the chiseled features of his face.

Weeks ago, I didn't really see Samuel whenever I looked at him, except in his eyes.

Now, I started to see pieces of the man he once was. In the deep furrow of his brow. In the firm and unyielding line of his lips. In the tense set of his jaw.

My fingers trailed to a long, thin scar running along the side of his ribs. "And this one?"

His silence stretched for so long I thought he wouldn't answer. Maybe he couldn't remember.

Then he said, "His name was Carlos. It was his first fight. He couldn't have been much older than eighteen."

As he spoke, his gaze grew distant. His body may lay next to mine, but his mind was far away. Still trapped in that hellhole that deprived him of so much more than just four years of his life.

"The kid was scrawny. Terrified. But he fought like hell. He knew what would happen if he didn't." A subtle laugh fell from his throat. "He reminded me of some of the kids I taught martial arts at the community center. He had that same look in his eyes."

"What happened?" I asked, even though I already knew. If Gideon was here, there was only one possible outcome.

"He got in a lucky shot with a piece of metal, but that was all. It didn't take much for me to knock him out. They started shouting at me to kill him, but..." He broke off, his throat working as he swallowed hard. "I couldn't do it. *Wouldn't* do it. I was so tired of playing their game."

He sucked in a deep breath, his grip on me tightening, as if he needed me to keep him grounded. To remind him I was here. That he survived.

"So they strung us up like pigs about to be slaughtered and whipped us until one of us died."

I covered my mouth with my hand, trying to stifle the sound of my choked sob. I'd seen the marks on his back. Knew what they were probably from. But hearing the full extent of his torture was almost unbearable.

"What was your first fight like?" I asked, despite a voice in my head telling me to change the subject to something lighter. Happier.

But we needed to do this. Needed to talk about it. Needed to normalize the trauma of his past.

"Terrifying."

I squeezed my eyes shut, a lump building in my

throat. I couldn't even begin to imagine what that must have felt like.

"I'd been training for a few weeks at that time. I'd been forced to watch the fights and had seen other men take their last breath. But nothing could have prepared me to be in that cage. To hear the guard order us to pick up our weapons and remind us that the match would only end when one of us was dead. All I was given was an empty beer bottle while my opponent had spiked knuckle dusters. I thought for sure I'd die. There was no way I could kill someone with a beer bottle."

"How did you?"

"It's still foggy. I guess my will to live was greater than his."

I heard the guilt still lingering in his voice, even after all this time. Winning meant surviving, but it also meant taking a life. Even in the fights where he walked away without physical scars, I knew the mental scars went far deeper. He'd carry those the rest of his life.

"That happened a lot," he continued. "After someone had been there a while, at some point they just gave up. Would rather die than continue living in that hell. Wanted to go out on their own terms. No one else's."

I grabbed his hand, intertwining our fingers. "But not you."

He peered down at me, bringing my hand to his lips and feathering a soft kiss to the skin.

"I guess I had something to live for." He gently pushed me onto my back, his touch achingly soft as he smoothed a few strands of hair away from my face before cupping my cheek.

It was such a contrast from the way he fucked me last night, leaving me sore in all the right places. But despite being drawn to his darkness, I was also drawn to his light. To his heart. To his soul.

"I had *you* to live for, Imogene," he murmured against my mouth. "Swear you won't ever let me forget that again."

"Never," I promised as he touched his lips to mine.

I pulled him closer, our bodies molding together as we deepened the exchange. The taste of his tongue as it swiped against mine was like a forbidden fruit, intoxicating and addictive. But even with his body flush with mine, it wasn't enough. I needed more of him.

Needed *all* of him.

As if able to read my innermost thoughts, he settled between my thighs, bringing his erection up to my entrance. Without breaking his lips from mine, he pushed inside. A whimper escaped my throat at the sensation of completeness consuming me.

I circled my legs around his waist, drawing him closer with every gentle thrust, not wanting so much as a speck of air between us. He moved against me, slow and deliberate, sending waves of pleasure through my body.

This was exactly what I needed right now. I wanted him like this, laid bare and vulnerable. Accepting of his past and the role it would play in our present and future.

Accepting of his scars and faults.

He slowly pulled his lips away, his gaze locked on mine as our bodies continued their sensual dance. The depth of emotion in his eyes sent a thrill through me, my heart swelling with love for this man. For every part of him — his darkness, his light, and all the gray areas in between.

I ran my fingers along his arms, exploring each and every scar, until my hand came to rest over his heart. It beat steadily beneath my touch, a strong and constant rhythm despite the weight of his past.

"Mine," I whispered hoarsely.

He nodded, trailing his own hand to cover my heart. "Mine."

We sealed our promise with a kiss, neither one of us removing our hands as we savored in our connection. In our devotion. In our love.

Each thump of our hearts, each hitch of our breaths, each moan of pleasure felt like a sacred ritual, solidifying our bond and reaffirming our unwavering commitment to each other.

No matter what the future held.

CHAPTER TWENTY-THREE

Imogene

"I hope this meets your expectations," Gideon said as he swung open the door to our hotel room, revealing a luxurious suite with sleek, modern furniture and floor-to-ceiling windows that offered an unparalleled view of the ocean shimmering in the afternoon sunlight.

I stepped inside, my gaze sweeping across the living area, taking in every detail. From the marble-topped bar to the plush sectional that beckoned me to sink into its soft cushions, especially after traveling across the country, albeit in a private plane.

Beyond a set of elegant French doors, the bedroom awaited us with its king-sized bed adorned in crisp white linens that practically gleamed.

"I suppose it'll do."

Facing him, I draped an arm over his shoulder and lifted myself onto my toes, brushing my lips against his.

"It's no Seaside Motel, but I'll make the most out of it."

He threw his head back and laughed, the sound echoing in the space.

In the early days of our relationship, nearly all of Gideon's money had been tied up in his gaming platform. Whenever we were able to sneak away for a weekend at the beach, the places we stayed weren't exactly five-star, luxurious resorts. Back then, staying in a place like this had been a distant dream, one we'd shared on quiet nights when the only sounds were the ocean waves and Ollie snoring at our feet.

"I hope it won't be too much of an inconvenience."

"Certainly not," I said as he pressed his mouth more firmly against mine, gently coaxing my lips to part.

Weeks ago, I didn't think this was possible. Hell, just a few days ago, I didn't think it was. Thought he'd punish himself for the rest of his life. Thought each day, more and more pieces of Gideon Saint would disappear until I was left with a man I didn't recognize.

That was no longer the case. I finally had everything I wanted. Samuel's loving nature. Gideon's intense passion. And this new man he was because of everything he'd been through. Everything he'd survived.

"Come on. Let's check out the view," he suggested.

"Lead the way," I replied.

Placing a hand on the small of my back, he steered me toward the balcony. The sliding glass doors opened up to an expansive view of the ocean, its waves crashing against the shore in a hypnotic rhythm.

As we stepped outside, the salty sea air enveloped me, invigorating me. A pair of wooden patio chairs sat facing the breathtaking scenery, a table between them. And placed on that table was an ice bucket with a bottle of champagne in it. An expensive one, too.

"Thirsty?" Gideon retrieved the bottle from the ice and skillfully removed the cage around the cork.

"I'll never turn down bubbles. Especially a delicious bottle like that."

"That's my girl," he said with a smirk, twisting the cork until it popped.

"I love that sound," I remarked, watching as he carefully poured the effervescent liquid into a flute.

"Me, too. Almost as much as the sound you make when you come," he added coolly, as if he were talking about the weather.

Regardless, it still made my cheeks heat.

"Play your cards right, and you might just hear both sounds in one day."

"Oh, I *definitely* plan on hearing both sounds in one day," he replied, handing me a flute.

"What should we drink to?"

He pinched his lips together, a contemplative look crossing his brow. "How about the future? *Our* future?"

"To our future," I said, gently touching my glass to his.

"Our future," he echoed, his eyes never leaving mine as we each took a sip of our champagne.

"I hope it's to your liking."

"Because *Dom Perignon* is so disgusting," I retorted sarcastically, stepping toward the railing and allowing the comforting ocean breeze to blow through my hair. "It's seriously a chore to drink it."

Smirking, I brought my glass to my lips, fighting to swallow back the moan wanting to be set free from the smooth flavor. A girl could certainly get used to this.

"Remember the *Opus One* bottle?" I asked after a comfortable silence as we simply enjoyed being back in this place that was home to so many memories.

He set his flute on the railing and flashed me a gentle smile I felt deep in my soul. "How can I forget?"

When he was laid off from his programming job, he went to the liquor store and bought a ridiculously expensive bottle of wine. You'd think after being laid off, he'd want to save as much money as possible, but he saw being laid off as a blessing. As his chance to finally devote all his time and effort to the gaming platform he'd been working on with Liam. He bought that bottle as a symbol of the life he wanted to live, the success he hoped to achieve.

Even after we finished that bottle of wine, we didn't get rid of it. Instead, we continued to drink out of it, filling it with whatever cheap wine we had on hand, usually from a box. Some of my happiest memories with him included that bottle as we'd eat ramen noodles while pretending to be dining at a Michelin-starred restaurant.

He didn't have lofty dreams of the wealth he had now, unlike Liam. Instead, all he wanted was to be comfortable. I prayed that was all the future held for us. Nothing but comfort.

"Did you ever think you'd get here?" I mused absent-mindedly. "That *we'd* get here?"

He turned toward me and wrapped me in his embrace before tipping my eyes to meet his. "Honestly, I'm still waiting for the bottom to fall, especially after everything. For years, my life was hell on earth, Imogene. The things I saw... The things I had to do to survive..."

"But you *did* survive." I placed my hand against his cheek. "That's all that matters."

He curved closer. "Yes, it is."

When his mouth touched mine in a soft kiss, I sighed, his affection seeping into me.

For the first time in what felt like forever, I felt a flicker of hope — not just for us, but for a future. Where the weight of the past didn't loom so heavily over us.

But as much as I wanted to believe we were finally on our way back to the dream we once shared, there were still too many unanswered questions to ignore the uneasy feeling settling in my stomach. Like a storm was brewing offshore, gathering strength before wreaking havoc.

I hoped I was wrong.

CHAPTER TWENTY-FOUR

Gideon

The early light crept through the gauzy curtains, soft and golden, casting a gentle glow over the room. The rhythmic sound of the waves crashing outside mingled with Imogene's soft, steady breaths as she slept in my arms. For a moment, I allowed myself to forget about everything else — Liam, Agent Myers, the ghosts of my past.

Here, in this moment, in our bubble, there was no guilt. No reminder of who I'd been or what I'd done.

There was only her.

Imogene stirred slightly, her body radiating warmth and softness. Her silky blonde hair brushed against my chin as she nuzzled into me, as if drawn to me even in her dreams. I couldn't resist pulling her closer still, savoring every delicious curve of her body.

I'd gone years without holding her like this. Without *touching* her like this.

Now that she was back in my arms where she belonged, I didn't want to stop. Didn't want another day to pass without having her in my bed. In my heart. In my life.

My fingers moved of their own accord, tracing the intricate lines of the tattoo on her hip — the symbol of unconditional love.

I'd first drawn this very symbol on her during one of our weekend escapes here. I still remembered the day vividly, as if it was only yesterday. How I'd held her just like this after making love to her, unable to stop touching her, tracing the symbol over and over.

The day I first noticed her tattoo was like a punch to the gut. I'd been convinced she'd forgotten me. That she didn't care about me. I was content with my plan to use her to get close to Liam and the rest of the men who'd betrayed me, then toss her out like the garbage I thought she was.

This tattoo changed everything. It was proof that I hadn't been entirely erased from her life. That she still loved me.

Now we both bore the same symbol as a testament of our love and devotion to each other.

"This might be my favorite way to wake up," she murmured sleepily.

I couldn't help but smile at her words as I propped myself up on one elbow to look down at her. "What? With a view of the ocean? Pretty sure you have that in California, too."

She shifted to face me, pushing back a few tendrils of my dark hair. "No. Here. With you."

I touched a soft kiss to her lips. "It's mine, too."

"Don't get me wrong," she added quickly. "I love the house in Del Mar. But out here..." She floated her gaze toward the floor-to-ceiling windows overlooking the eastern shoreline. "It's less hectic. More peaceful."

"Then let's move here," I suggested without a moment's hesitation.

Her eyes widened. "Here?"

"Or anywhere else you want. I think after everything we've been through, we both deserve somewhere peaceful. I know the surfing is better on the west coast, and Melanie's there, but they're both a quick flight away." I grabbed her hand in mine, bringing it up to my lips. "I just want you to be happy."

"*You* make me happy." She inched closer and pressed a kiss to my mouth. "But I do like the idea of living here. Or at least closer to Mama and Lachlan now that I'm not running from ghosts anymore."

She shifted her body, settling into my arms as I held

her tight, both of us watching the sun slowly rise over the horizon, casting a warm glow over everything in sight.

Neither one of us said anything for quite a while. Instead, we basked in each other as we watched the sky change colors, everything about this moment perfect. This was what I wanted. A quiet life with her by my side. I just prayed it was still in the cards for us.

"What's the plan for today?" she asked several minutes later.

"I've got a beautiful woman naked in my bed and the perfect view of the ocean. What else is there?"

"What else indeed," she murmured as her lips found mine once more, her tongue swiping against mine.

"Actually, I booked you a spa appointment after lunch," I said once she brought the kiss to an end. "Massage. Manicure. Pedicure. The works."

She furrowed her brow. "But we came out here to spend time together. How can we spend time together if I'm at the spa all afternoon?"

"We have four more days to do absolutely nothing if you'd like. But I wanted to treat you to a bit of pampering today. Figured you deserved it after the past few weeks. Plus, it'll give me time to arrange the little surprise I have planned for later on."

Her eyes sparkled with a mixture of excitement and curiosity. "A surprise?"

My smile grew, and I nodded.

"What is it?"

"If I told you, it wouldn't be a surprise," I teased.

"That's not fair," she pouted, falling onto her back in mock frustration. "You know this is going to drive me crazy all day."

"That's the point. What good is surprising you if I can't torture you about it beforehand?"

"We'll see who's torturing who."

Before I could react, she straddled me and pinned my arms on either side of my head. Her hair cascaded around us as she leaned in close, our breaths intermingling.

"Come on, Gideon," she whispered seductively. "Tell me. I'll make it worth your while." She trailed her tongue along my unshaven jawline before taking my earlobe between her teeth and nibbling.

"You're going to have to try harder than that to get me to talk," I ground out, despite how turned on I was.

"Is that a challenge?"

I playfully waggled my brows. "Maybe."

"Well then..." She sensually rolled her hips against me, my erection throbbing at the heat between her legs. "Challenge accepted."

I groaned, gripping her hips as I met her rhythm, wanting nothing more than to sink deep inside of her, despite the fact that we spent most of last night doing this precise thing. Her lips hovered over mine, but every time I craned toward them in an attempt to capture them, she moved just out of reach, remaining close enough to make me lose my mind.

"You're not playing fair, Imogene."

Her mouth tipped into a mischievous smirk. "Then tell me the surprise."

"Not a chance in hell."

I used her brief moment of frustration to my advantage, flipping her onto her back so she was beneath me.

"Now who's not playing fair?" she whimpered as I slowly pulsed against her, my erection hitting her clit.

"I never promised to play fair. In fact, I think you like it when I don't." I wrapped my hands around her wrists and pinned them against her head, leaving her completely at my mercy. "Am I right?" I arched a single brow as I teased her opening with my cock.

"God, yes," she exhaled, her eyes rolling into the back of her head.

"That's what I thought," I responded before slamming into her, fucking any thought of today's surprise right out of her.

There was no doubt in my mind. This was my favorite way to wake up, too.

CHAPTER TWENTY-FIVE

Imogene

The clock ticked closer to six, each second feeling like an eternity as I anxiously waited for Gideon's return. He told me to be ready at six for my surprise, but now I couldn't help but worry about where he might be. What if something happened to him?

What if Liam somehow found us? Found him?

My mind raced with all the possibilities, each scenario worse than the one before.

I reached for my phone to text him when a knock on the door startled me. Maybe it was Gideon.

Why would he knock when he had a key? Then again, maybe it was part of the surprise he'd planned.

Placing my cell in my purse, I checked my reflection

in the mirror one last time, smoothing my hands down my sundress. I wasn't sure what to expect tonight, but Gideon told me to wear something nice, yet comfortable. So a sundress it was.

The fabric swished around me as I walked to the door and peered through the peephole.

But it wasn't Gideon. Instead, a man in a hotel uniform stood in the hallway, holding an envelope.

"Can I help you?" I asked, opening the door cautiously.

"Good evening, Ms. Prescott. This is for you." He handed me the envelope. "Enjoy your evening."

All I could do was nod in return, curious yet relieved, especially when I saw Gideon's unmistakable sharp, slanted script.

Shutting the door behind me, I slipped my finger under the flap and unfolded the paper inside.

> *Our journey begins where the ocean meets the shore,*
> *Where sunlight dances upon waves forever more.*
> *We etched a story in sand, hearts alight,*
> *Return to that spot near the jetty rocks tonight.*

> *P.S. - There's a driver waiting in the lobby*
> *to take you wherever you need to go.*

A smile spread on my lips as memories flooded back from a birthday years ago when Gideon surprised me with a scavenger hunt around Atlanta. Or Samuel did. But they were no longer two separate entities. They were the same.

As I sat in the back of a dark sedan, the driver Gideon hired chatted amiably while I attempted to reel in my excitement over what might be waiting for me at the end of the scavenger hunt. But I didn't want to rush this. I wanted to enjoy this journey. Savor each meticulously planned clue.

Less than ten minutes later, the driver dropped me off near a beach access road that led to the jetty. I climbed out and headed toward the sound of crashing waves. Removing my shoes, I relished in the feel of the cool sand between my toes. It always comforted me. Reminded me of the early mornings in Hawaii when Lachlan and I would surf together.

The wind whipped strands of hair around my face as I trekked along the shoreline. In the distance, a series of large rocks lined the sand and continued into the ocean.

During high tide, they were often hidden beneath the water, but it was low tide now, giving me the perfect view of the various rocks, pelicans and seagulls perched on top, preening their feathers with graceful movements.

I scanned the area, unsure what I was looking for. If this was anything like the last scavenger hunt, Gideon would have left me a clue somewhere.

But where?

I continued searching, knowing he would have made it obvious but not overly conspicuous. Then I saw it. A cork.

But not just any cork.

It belonged to a bottle of *Opus One* Cabernet Sauvignon.

Grinning to myself, I picked it up, revealing a small note tied to it that had been buried in the sand. I quickly untied it with the enthusiasm of a kid at Christmas so I could read the next clue.

> *It wasn't the trinket but laughter we shared,*
> *In a shop where the scent of the ocean hung near.*
> *Among treasures of shells and souvenirs bright,*
> *Find the place where I knew you were my light.*

Shoving the cork and the clue into my purse, I darted back down the beach, hopping into my chauffeured car and telling the driver where to go.

When I arrived at the souvenir shop that Gideon and I would always visit, regardless of how tacky the merchandise was, I wandered through aisles of over-priced trinkets and cheesy t-shirts. This place was almost exactly as I remembered it, right down to the gaudy dish-towels that said "You're Shore Acting Like a Beach Today".

As I passed a rack of personalized license plate keychains, I nearly continued walking, but something made me stop.

My fingers skimmed the rows, half-smiling at the old annoyance of never finding my name on anything like this. Not with a name like Imogene.

But then I froze.

There it was — a keychain with my name.

And attached to it was another rolled-up piece of paper.

On a bench for two as the light softly fell,
Where the colors of dusk cast their radiant spell.
A promise was formed, though unspoken it stayed,

Return to the spot where my heart was swayed.

I knew where to go in a heartbeat. One of our favorite spots — a bench at the ruins of an old plantation.

From there, Gideon's clues led me across the island, each stop like flipping through an old scrapbook filled with memories. From the beach where we'd once shared ice cream, fighting against the wind and each other for every last lick. To the kayak rental shop where he'd teased me about my terrible paddling form, his laughter echoing in the air even though he wasn't with me.

As I followed the clues, I felt myself falling more and more in love with him, my anticipation building with each stop to the point that I almost didn't want this game to end. But when I found a clue near our favorite seafood restaurant, I knew it was about to.

Where light meets the sky, a tower so bright,
The place where we saw our future take flight.
Climb up the tower, where promises grew,
And the horizon became our shared view.

There was no question in my mind the search was

taking me to the Harbour Town Lighthouse, one of Hilton Head's most famous spots.

And with the sun about to set, I knew exactly where I'd find him. At the very top.

But even after I climbed over a hundred steps, he wasn't there. Maybe I was wrong. Maybe he meant for his clue to lead me somewhere else. But where? Was there another tower I'd forgotten about?

Just as I was about to head back to the bottom, I spied a napkin on the floor.

If this were any other time, I wouldn't give it a second thought. But considering it bore the logo of the beachside seafood shack from a few clues ago, I darted toward it. As expected, when I turned it over, there was yet another clue. The final one.

> *This treasure hunt ends where it all took flight,*
> *In the room that welcomed us last night.*
> *Come find me there, where the view meets the sea,*
> *And together, we'll write the next chapter of our history.*

After hurrying down all those stairs as fast as my legs could carry me, I hopped back in the car, my heart hammering every second of the drive back to the hotel. It felt like it took an eternity instead of the mere minutes that actually passed.

By the time I reached the suite, my palms were damp with nerves. I hesitated in the hallway for a second, trying to steady my breathing.

Then I held the key card up to the pad and opened the door, stopping dead in my tracks at the sight that greeted me.

CHAPTER TWENTY-SIX

Imogene

I hesitated in the doorway, taking it all in. The room I'd left mere hours ago was now unrecognizable, transformed into a romantic dreamscape straight out of a fairy tale. Soft candlelight flickered across every surface, the golden glow bouncing off the floor-to-ceiling windows and casting gentle shadows on the walls. The faint scent of roses and sea salt hung in the air, as if the very essence of the island had been bottled and poured into the room.

My footsteps echoed against the polished floor as I made my way inside. A trail of crimson rose petals wound its way through the suite like an invitation. The music of a gentle guitar drifted through the air — calm, soothing, yet achingly familiar. It was a melody I often heard Samuel play.

The balcony door was open, the sheer curtains swaying in the evening breeze. It carried with it the faint crash of the ocean waves and the crisp tang of salt, mingling with the soothing aroma from the candles. My chest tightened as I followed the petals, drawn as much to the setting as I was to the overwhelming anticipation curling low in my stomach.

As I stepped outside, a smile spread across my lips at the sight that greeted me.

Gideon stood by the railing, silhouetted against the horizon where the last streaks of dusk melted into the inky sky. He wore a sharp navy suit that fit him perfectly, though he'd skipped the tie. The open collar added a touch of ease to his otherwise commanding presence. The perfect combination of Gideon and Samuel. But it was the look in his eyes that rooted me to the spot — so much love and devotion, it left me completely breathless.

"Are you my reward?" I managed to ask, despite my racing heart.

"I hope so," he replied as he stepped toward me. His voice was low and intimate, full of raw emotion that sent shivers down my spine.

But before I could utter a single syllable in response, he reached into his pocket and gracefully dropped to one knee.

The world around us instantly vanished, leaving only the two of us and the sound of our hearts beating as one.

"Imogene..." His voice was thick with emotion as he took my hand in his. "I never thought I'd get to do this. For four years, I took it day by day. Hour by hour. Minute by minute. Every day, I woke up fully prepared for it to be my last."

I swallowed hard, a tear sliding down my cheek at how terrifying that must have been. Yet, he somehow managed to find the strength to survive. To not give up.

"When I finally escaped, I almost ruined it all over again. I let revenge consume me. In my mind, it was the only way to settle the score. But I don't want to live like that anymore. Not when I have a chance at something better. At something real."

He opened a small velvet box and revealed a sparkling, round-cut solitaire diamond. It was simple, but elegant. Just like him.

"I don't want to be defined by what happened to me, by the mistakes I've made." His voice softened, his eyes piercing into mine. "I want to be defined by *you*, Imogene. By us. By this love I didn't think I'd ever find again. All that time I was locked away, I thought my need for revenge kept me alive. Now that I'm able to think clearly again, I've realized I was wrong. *You* kept me alive. Your love. Your refusal to give up on me. It brought me back from hell. *You* brought me back from hell."

My heart swelled with gratitude that our love had been strong enough to see him through his darkest days. It helped me through mine, too, even if I didn't realize it at the time.

"I've been looking back for too long. I'm not going to do that anymore. Orpheus lost Eurydice because he looked back. I won't lose you because of it."

He paused for a beat, taking a deep breath to settle his emotions.

"I may not know what the future holds. But I do know I want to spend it with you. Every second. Every moment."

"Gideon..." I exhaled, struggling to blink away the tears spilling from my eyelids.

"I know it's not an extravagant ring," he continued before I could attempt to make sense of everything I was feeling.

He gave me a heartwarming smile that was a mixture of Samuel, Gideon, and every other part of this man I couldn't imagine not having in my life.

"When the gaming platform took off and I started making real money, the first thing I did was go to a jewelry store and buy this ring. I knew we were nowhere near that stage of our relationship. I figured since the wine bottle worked for my professional life, buying a ring might work for us. Luckily Henry thought to keep it so I can do what I've wanted for too long now."

He licked his lips, his eyes locked on mine with love and determination. "I know there's a lot left unresolved, but I also know just how fleeting life can be. I don't want to waste another second of my life without you by my side."

His voice cracked slightly as he brought the ring up to my finger and whispered, "Imogene, will you marry me?"

I shook my head, tears blurring my vision as I stared down at this beautiful, imperfect man.

I once imagined what it would be like if he proposed. Truthfully, I wasn't sure if it would ever happen, not when we were trying to keep our relationship hidden from Liam. Or, more accurately, *I* was trying to keep it from Liam.

When I got that phone call and learned Samuel was presumed dead after his car was found with a bullet hole in the blood-soaked driver's seat, my biggest regret was loving him in the shadows. Like he just said... We had a second chance. I wasn't going to ruin this, regardless of the uncertainties that loomed ahead.

"Please say something," he begged after several long moments, the silence between us heavy. Then a smile lit up my face.

"How does yes sound?" I choked out.

Relief covered his expression as he slid the ring onto my finger and jumped to his feet, pulling my body against his. "Yes sounds fucking perfect."

His lips found mine, warm and urgent, and I melted into him. With each touch of his hands against my skin, a soft sigh escaped my lips.

In this moment, I didn't allow myself to worry about all the uncertainties hovering like a foreboding cloud in the distance. Instead, I let myself believe we could have this. That we could be happy. That we could live the life we once dreamed of.

"Hold on," he warned after bringing the kiss to an end.

"What do you mean?"

He swooped me into his arms and carried me inside. The warmth of his body radiated through me as he held me close, making my heart race in anticipation.

He reached the bedroom in just a handful of strides, carefully setting me down. But he didn't let go. His hands caressed me as he walked me backwards toward the bed, his lips moving sensually against mine in a kiss that felt like it could mend all the cracks and fissures inside me.

He moved from my mouth, peppering kisses along my jawline and down the column of my neck before spinning me around. He tugged the tie of my dress loose and it fell to the floor, my bra and panties soon joining it.

Facing him, I pushed his jacket off his shoulders, my eyes locking with his as I slowly unbuttoned his shirt. I couldn't help but marvel at how far we'd come since the first time I tried to do this same thing and he stopped me. It seemed so long ago. Like we were different people back then, despite it only being a few short months ago.

Then again, we *were* different people back then. Gideon was still clinging to the past. In a way, so was I, still in love with a ghost.

But now, as I ran my hands over the same scars I did that day, I found myself appreciating them even more. Every mark, every line, every bump made him into who he was today. But it didn't define him. Even better, he wasn't *letting* them define him anymore.

Once he stepped out of his shoes and his clothes joined mine, he steered me toward the bed, carefully lowering me onto the surface.

His mouth captured mine again, his kiss so deep and full of emotion it took everything in me not to break into tears. We'd shared so many moments during our time together, both before and now. But this moment, knowing he was finally mine, that we finally made it to this point, it was so much bigger than I thought possible.

"Please," I begged, wrapping my legs around his waist and circling my hips.

"What do you need?" he rasped, burying his head in the crook of my neck, teeth nipping, tongue teasing.

"You, Gideon." I held his face in my hands. "Always you."

Without breaking eye contact, he slid inside of me.

There were no punishing thrusts or desperate drives. Instead, he took his time, savoring me inch by inch, letting me feel all of him. Letting me *see* all of him.

It was almost too much. But at the same time, it wasn't enough.

When he was fully seated, he stayed there for several long moments, his face pinched, as if he was struggling to contain all the sensations consuming him.

Then he exhaled, all the tension rolling off him in waves. He captured my mouth, his tongue swiping against mine in a tantalizingly slow rhythm that matched the way he currently pushed in and out of me.

I held him close as we chased our bliss, our bodies working in perfect harmony until we both fell over the edge together.

CHAPTER TWENTY-SEVEN

Gideon

I leaned against the wet bar in the back yard of Imogene's parents' Atlanta home, unable to tear my eyes from her as she sat beside her mother on a wicker couch. The warm summer sun cast a golden glow over everything, from the sparkling pool to the lush green grass. Imogene's laughter, that light, airy sound I hadn't heard enough of in the past few weeks, rang out over the conversation. For a moment, it eased something deep inside me.

As much as I enjoyed the idea of staying in Hilton Head forever, it wasn't reality. Imogene had been cleared to return to work, so we needed to get back to California.

But we needed to stop in Atlanta first. I promised as much when I called Imogene's mom and stepfather to ask for their permission to marry her. Honestly, I didn't think they'd agree, not when they knew the truth about who I was.

To my surprise, they didn't voice a single hesitation. Instead, they thanked me for asking them, but said Imogene was an adult and they trusted her judgment to do what she believed was in her best interests.

Lucky for me, she said yes.

I should have been happy. In many ways, I was. But there was still that niggle of worry in the back of my mind, the one whispering that I didn't deserve this. That all of this could be taken away.

"I don't think I've seen her smile this much in ages." Henry's voice cut through the haze of my thoughts, and I snapped my attention away from Imogene, meeting his eyes. "It's good to see her happy."

"Yes, it is." I brought my scotch up to my mouth.

"It's good to see you happy, too. Now that you've finally pulled your head out of your ass."

I chuckled and raised my glass in a mock salute. "Thanks to you."

"You would have figured it out eventually. I'm just glad I could give you the push you needed."

"Thanks, brother." I passed him a genuine smile, grateful for his constant support.

"Anytime." He held my gaze for a beat before

clearing his throat and lowering his voice. "I did some digging into that FBI agent like you asked."

The mention of Agent Myers brought me back to reality. The past few days had been such a blur. Not to mention, it felt like Imogene and I were living in a bubble, so far removed from our worries.

Now we were back in the real world again. With it, came the reminder of all the problems still facing us.

"What did you find?" I asked, trying to mask the anxiety creeping into my voice.

"It's not much," he admitted, his tone apologetic. "But he went to the same college as Brian McGuire. They were even in the same forensics class about thirty years ago. Apparently, McGuire was a criminal justice major before he switched to mortuary science."

"So what if they were in the same class thirty years ago?" I argued. "It could just be a coincidence."

While I struggled to believe anything was merely a coincidence, the connection was tenuous. With what was at stake, I couldn't jump to conclusions.

"I'll keep digging, see if there's been any recent connection between the two."

I nodded, unsure if I wanted him to find anything. "Thanks."

"I'll let you get back to your soon-to-be wife." He chuckled under his breath. "Never thought I'd see the day."

"You and me both." I threw him a wink, then started toward where Imogene sat with her mom, Melanie, and Melanie's mother, Olivia. I could hear them talk about wedding plans all the way over here.

I didn't care where we got married. All I *did* care about was making her my wife. Becoming her husband. It was a strange thought, considering where I was mere months ago.

Imogene changed all that.

Just like she had all those years ago, too.

"Gideon," a commanding voice called out, forcing me to come to a stop.

Turning, I met Alexander Burnham's hardened eyes, causing a hint of unease to flow through me.

Despite the polite conversation we all shared over the past few hours as we celebrated my and Imogene's engagement, I still felt him studying me with scrutiny.

Just like he did the last time I saw him in Pebble Beach.

But I was no longer hiding who I was, worried if anyone might see past the lies, it would be the highly trained former Navy SEAL.

Instead, everyone here knew the truth — that I was once Samuel Tate before the men I trusted betrayed me.

"Mr. Burnham, sir," I greeted Melanie's father respectfully.

"Congratulations." He extended his hand toward me

and we shook briefly. "It should come as no surprise that I think of Imogene as a second daughter."

"Of course, sir."

"I'm happy for her. For both of you. You deserve this."

"We do?"

His words took me by surprise. After all, he now knew I'd lied to him. To all of them. While everyone else seemed ready to overlook my actions, I didn't think Alexander would.

"Yes." His lips curved into a slight smile as he brought his scotch to his mouth. Then his gaze drifted toward his wife, his expression lightening. "I know better than anyone that sometimes you need to keep secrets in order to keep those you love safe."

I nodded in understanding.

While I may have had less than altruistic motives when I started down this path, that changed along the way. My actions weren't solely out of revenge, but also to protect Imogene. To remove any and all threats to her safety.

Myself included.

"What's your plan for Liam Pierce?"

I darted my eyes back to his, unsure how to respond.

While everyone knew who I was now, I hadn't shared the details of everything I'd done.

Then again, I shouldn't have been surprised that

Alexander Burnham would be the one to put all the pieces together.

Much like Agent Myers did.

But Agent Myers didn't know with certainty who I really was. His theory was just that... A theory. Even if it did hit quite close to the truth.

"You don't need to cover for yourself," Alexander continued. "I've been around long enough to read between the lines."

"And what did you find between the lines?" I asked evenly, not wanting to give anything away.

"That you haven't merely been sitting idly by, hoping all those assholes finally paid for what they did to you. That you took matters into your own hands."

I didn't immediately confess. But I didn't deny his statement, either.

"I don't blame you. If I were in your shoes..." He shook his head as he took another long sip from his drink. "I'm not sure I would have been as patient or methodical about it. I wanted to let you know I understand." He narrowed his gaze on me. "There's what's legal. And then there's what's just. As long as you're on the side of justice, I'm with you. Whatever you need, I'll have your back."

"I appreciate the support, sir," I replied, "but this is my fight. I started it myself. If necessary, I'll end it myself."

Alexander briefly studied me before relaxing his posture. "Fair enough. But the offer stands. I can have trained mercenaries on-site within the hour."

"I hope it doesn't come to that."

"Me, too. But if it does, you know where to find me."

I offered him my thanks again before excusing myself and making my way toward Imogene, my heart warming at how beautiful and carefree she looked, her smile as radiant as the diamond now gracing her finger. The sight eased some of the tension Alexander's words had left behind. But only a little.

As I approached, Imogene instinctively reached for my hand, pulling me to sit beside her.

"I thought you got lost," she joked.

"Not lost." I glanced toward Alexander as he joined us. "Just sidetracked."

"Everything okay?" Imogene asked in a quiet voice, her gaze searching.

I touched a soft kiss to her forehead. "Never better."

"Good."

"Now that we finally have everyone out here," Melanie interjected, pushing herself to her feet. "If I could have your attention for a moment?"

The chatter quieted, and we all looked her way. She stood tall, her champagne glass held high, her expression full of warmth and pride.

"I'm so happy to be here to celebrate two of the most

important people in my life," Melanie began, beaming at Imogene. "It's been an emotional journey to get to this point. But if there's one thing I've always believed about Imogene, it's that she's one of the strongest people I've ever met. She holds her cards close, keeps her heart guarded. But when she lets someone in, she gives them everything."

She turned her attention fully to me, her voice softening.

"And that's exactly what she's given the man beside her... Everything. Even when the rest of us thought there was no way forward, she refused to let go of what she felt in her heart. She held on to hope when it would have been so much easier to give up. That hope is what brought you back to her, Gideon."

Imogene's fingers tightened around mine, and I glanced at her, my heart expanding as I caught the faint shimmer in her eyes.

"I won't pretend to understand everything you've both been through

to get here," Melanie continued, her voice growing steadier. "I don't think a single person on the planet could ever do that. But here's what I do know... The love you share is rare. It's the kind of love that endures. That overcomes. That transforms."

Her smile widened, her gaze sweeping over the

handful of people we felt compelled to invite to celebrate with today.

"So here's to Imogene and Gideon. To a love that doesn't just survive. It thrives. To the future they're building together. And to the happiness that's waiting for them."

The group echoed her toast, the soft clinking of glasses filling the air. Imogene turned to me, her smile as bright as the sun, and I leaned in to brush a kiss to her lips.

"I love you," I murmured.

"And I love you."

But as she pressed another kiss to my mouth, the knot in my chest returned.

Melanie's words had been perfect — poignant, heartfelt, and full of hope.

Hope I wanted to believe in.

But I'd learned long ago how fleeting hope could be.

I feared it would soon be taken from us, too.

CHAPTER TWENTY-EIGHT

Imogene

Packing up my townhouse wasn't as bittersweet as I'd expected.

After all, it never truly felt like home.

When I moved to California earlier this year, I thought it would be the fresh start I needed. That it would somehow help me move on and forget the past.

Little did I know my past would soon find me.

Regardless, I never decluttered my life. Never let go of things.

That was what I was doing, especially now that Gideon and I were about to embark on the next chapter of our lives. Instead of simply stuffing all my belongings into boxes and taking them with me, I was finally going through everything, getting rid of anything I'd been holding on to for far too long.

It felt freeing to finally do this. To purge my life.

And with each item I discarded, it lightened the weight I'd been carrying.

This move wasn't just about consolidating space. It was about making room for something new.

When I couldn't fit anything else in the trash bag, I tied it up and pulled myself to my feet. My muscles were sore from all the lifting I'd been doing, but I pushed ahead.

Since I decided not to renew my lease on a townhouse I no longer lived in, I needed to be out by the end of the weekend so the property management company could prepare it for the new tenant.

Which was why I'd been coming here every day after work.

Gideon had been coming here to help after work, too.

Apparently, his cover story that he was a venture capitalist was actually true, much to my surprise. With all the money he now had after Henry gave him his share of the profits in his cyber security firm, Gideon wanted to do something with that money. It was his way of paying it forward, considering he wouldn't have found any success if an angel investor hadn't taken a risk on his concept for a gaming platform.

It was because of that success he was able to provide the start-up funds for Henry's firm.

Lifting the giant trash bag off the floor, I carried it onto the back deck and toward the trash bins tucked along the side of the detached garage. I heaved it on top of the other bags, the lid no longer able to fully close.

I brushed some of the dust off my shirt and yoga pants and was about to turn when a sound coming from the garage caught my attention, faint but noticeable.

Was someone in there? Or was I just letting my mind play tricks on me because of the recent break-in?

That had to be it. This townhouse was completely safe and secure. If anyone broke in while I wasn't here, I'd know.

More importantly, *Gideon* would know.

Reminding myself of that, I shook off my unease and started back toward the house.

Then I heard it again.

But this time, it was more than just a light shuffling sound. It was more deliberate. More rhythmic. Almost like footsteps against the cement floor of the garage.

I turned toward the building, every nerve in my body on edge. A million scenarios raced through my mind. Maybe it was a raccoon. Or a squirrel.

But it sounded too weighty to be an animal.

My heart hammering in my chest, I walked toward the door and placed my hand on the knob. With a steady inhale, I turned it, pushing the door open, unsure what I'd find.

But it was empty.

I stepped farther inside, my sneakers scuffing against the smooth floor, the sound unnervingly loud in the stillness. The garage smelled faintly of motor oil and damp concrete, the earthy scent mixing with a trace of mildew. The dim light filtering through the narrow windows cast uneven shadows across the floor, making the corners look darker and deeper than they were.

My eyes scanned the space, darting from one object to the next. The shelves lining the walls were cluttered but orderly — tools in neat rows, a box of Christmas decorations shoved to one side, a stack of old paint cans gathering dust that were here when I moved in.

I ran my hand along the workbench as I passed, the rough wood scraping against my skin. A few loose screws and nails clinked under my touch, but otherwise, everything seemed untouched. The only movement came from the faint swing of a cobweb dangling in the far corner.

Still, I couldn't shake the feeling that something wasn't right.

I crouched to look beneath the workbench, half-expecting to find a squirrel or maybe a stray cat that had wandered in. There was nothing except an old tarp and a forgotten paint roller.

As I stood, the air seemed to shift, a faint whisper of coolness brushing against my neck like a draft. I spun around, my pulse pounding in my ears as I searched the space yet again.

The shadows seemed to still, like they were holding their breath, waiting.

But for what?

"Hello?" I managed to say through the dryness in my throat, the taste of stale air lingering on my tongue.

The only response was the hum of the refrigerator and the sound of a lawn mower coming from down the street.

I forced myself to exhale, my breath shaky and shallow. I was being ridiculous. It was just my imagination magnifying every creak and shadow into something sinister.

But then I swore I heard it again — something soft, like the scrape of a shoe against concrete growing closer and closer.

Before I could spin around, a hand grabbed my arm, another clamping over my mouth. Panic surged through me as I struggled against whoever held me. I tried to remember my self-defense training. I knew I needed to calm down enough to think clearly, but that was easier said than done.

It didn't help that I hadn't kept up on my training. Plus, I was still regaining my strength after the accident.

I attempted to free myself, but his hold on me was too resolute.

Then I felt a sharp pain in my head, the world around me going fuzzy before everything went dark.

CHAPTER TWENTY-NINE

Gideon

"Imogene?"

My voice echoed as I walked into her townhouse, carrying a takeout bag in one hand and a bottle of wine in the other.

"Take a break for a minute. I brought sushi."

Setting the bag onto the kitchen island, I grabbed a couple of plates and glasses. I worked quickly, pouring the wine and arranging the sushi.

When Imogene still hadn't appeared by the time I finished, I called out to her again. But I didn't hear her footsteps. She probably had her earbuds in, completely absorbed in her audiobook or music. It wouldn't be the first time I'd have to track her down in her own house.

I made my way down the back hallway and toward

the office, peeking my head inside. It was empty. The boxes she'd packed up earlier this week were still lined up neatly against the wall, untouched since the last time I'd seen them.

Frowning, I climbed the stairs to the second floor. The door to her bedroom was open, and the subtle scent of her coconut body wash hung in the air. But the room was empty, too.

I glanced out the window, wondering if she was packing up the garage. While the automatic door was closed, the side door was cracked open.

I headed downstairs and continued onto the back deck, the wood creaking underneath my feet.

"Imogene," I called out as I approached the side of the detached garage, an uneasy feeling washing over me.

Something was off. But nothing appeared out of place. There was no sign of a break-in or struggle.

Shaking it off, I continued toward the side door and pushed it open, stepping into the dimly lit space.

The scent hit me first. Oil and dust, mixed with something faintly metallic. The garage was cooler than outside, the hum of the overhead light breaking the silence.

"Imogene?" I called again, my voice firmer now.

No response.

I scanned the space, taking in the rows of shelves

stocked with plastic bins, tools hung on the walls. Everything looked normal. Or it should have.

But the unease prickling at the back of my neck only grew.

I stepped farther inside, my shoes scuffing against the concrete.

That's when I saw it. A small, dark smear on the floor near the workbench.

I forced myself to move closer, my heart hammering as I crouched down. With a trembling hand, I reached out and touched the edge of the smear, coming away with a wet streak of crimson.

Blood.

Fresh.

A cold knot twisted in my stomach as I rose to my feet, my gaze darting across the space. My heart thumped loudly in my chest, drowning out any other noise as I searched the garage for answers. There were more droplets, faint but distinct, leading away from the bench and toward the automatic door.

I fought against the rising panic, telling myself there had to be an explanation. Maybe she'd cut herself while moving something. Maybe she'd gone inside to clean up, and I'd find her in the bathroom, annoyed that I was making a big deal out of nothing.

Gripping my phone, I called her as I dashed back inside, the tone ringing loud and relentless in my ear.

"Pick up, Imogene. Please."

I strained to hear it, hoping to catch the sound of her voice from somewhere in the house, despite having just searched it. Instead, it was silent except for the hum from the central air.

But then I heard it.

A subtle buzzing.

Not from the phone pressed to my ear, but from deeper inside the house.

I froze, my chest tightening as I followed the sound down the hallway and into the living room.

Imogene's phone sat on the coffee table, the screen lit up with my name. The harsh vibration rattled through the room, each pulse like a knife twisting inside of me.

My hand clenched around my own phone as the call disconnected, leaving the room eerily quiet.

I grabbed her cell, scanning it for any messages or calls. Nothing. The last text she'd sent was to me a few hours ago, telling me she was happy with sushi for dinner.

She promised me she wouldn't leave. That she'd keep the doors locked. That she'd be careful.

After everything that had happened — after Liam — I thought she understood how serious this was.

But the blood on the garage floor told a different story.

"Fuck!" I shouted, my voice raw with a mixture of

panic and fury. I paced back and forth, tugging at my hair as dozens of different scenarios played out in my mind.

If someone had taken her — if they'd *hurt* her — I would find them.

And I would make them pay.

I needed to think straight. Not let my emotions get the better of me. That was when people made mistakes. And there was too much at risk to make a mistake now.

Yanking my phone from my pocket, I called the one person who I knew would have a level head in this situation. Who always did, no matter what.

"She's gone," I blurted out before Henry could say anything in greeting.

"Slow down. What do you mean?"

"Imogene," I replied, my voice tight with barely restrained panic. It killed me to even say her name. It took everything I had not to weigh myself down with guilt over this.

If I'd left my last meeting when I was supposed to, I would have been here. I could have stopped all of this.

"What happened?" Henry asked, remaining collected as always.

"I've been helping her pack up her townhouse, but when I got here, she wasn't inside. The side door to the garage was open, so I figured maybe she was packing things up in there. When I went inside..." I swallowed hard. "I found blood. And no sign of Imogene except for her phone here in the living room. If she was safe…"

"Hang tight," Henry interjected. "I'm pulling up the cameras now." I could hear the rapid clacking of keys in the background. "Do you know what time she got to the townhouse?"

"I don't know." I paced the living room once more, feeling useless.

Every second I stayed here was a second wasted. Was another second whoever had Imogene could be taking her farther and farther away.

Could be harming her more.

"On non-game days, she usually leaves the stadium around five. I've been driving her and picking her up, but I had a meeting scheduled today, so she took one of my cars. I—"

"Don't put this on yourself," Henry admonished. "That won't do you any good right now. It won't do *Imogene* any good right now. Okay?"

I squeezed my eyes shut and nodded. "Okay."

"I'm sending a video to your phone from about thirty minutes ago."

I put him on speaker, then clicked on the message as it came in with the link to a video.

The footage displayed a wide shot from the back of Imogene's house, captured by one of the cameras. The garage stood to the right of the frame, its door closed and unassuming.

Within seconds, Imogene came into view, walking toward the trash bins with a bag in hand. She tossed it inside and turned back before stopping in her tracks. My heart hammered as I silently pleaded with her to keep walking. To continue into the house, even though I knew it wouldn't happen.

After several long moments, she turned back toward the garage and slowly approached it. She pulled the door wide and walked inside.

I held my breath, waiting for her to reappear. Five seconds passed. Ten.

"Come on, Imogene," I whispered.

Then a movement in the corner of the screen caught my attention. A man stepped into frame, emerging from the shadows of the backyard.

He was of average height and build, dressed in dark clothing, with a baseball hat pulled low, obscuring his face. He moved with purpose, his gait deliberate. He never once looked directly at the camera, as if he knew exactly where they were, making my blood run cold.

"Who the hell is that?" I demanded.

"I don't know," Henry replied. "He keeps his face completely hidden. My guess is he knows his way around surveillance. That's not random."

On the screen, the man made his way to the garage. He hesitated for a moment, then slipped inside.

I gritted my teeth, forcing myself to keep watching. But nothing else happened.

"I've got the driveway camera," Henry stated. "Sending it now."

I clicked on the link he sent from the camera on the exterior of the garage and saw a nondescript van reversing up to the garage door, stopping in a spot where he could have tossed Imogene into the back without the camera picking up on it.

As if he knew exactly where the blind spots were.

"Can you run the plate?" I asked frantically.

"There *is* no plate. He must have taken it off for this very reason."

I clenched my fists in frustration as I watched the same man jump out of the van and head into the back yard. After about five or so minutes, the man reappeared, climbed in behind the wheel, and drove away.

"Goddammit!" I shouted, desperation bubbling inside of me once more. I may not have seen him take Imogene, but the fact that she was last seen walking into a garage before disappearing didn't ease my mind.

"It's okay," Henry remarked. "We'll find her."

"How are we going to find her without a fucking license plate? How—"

"Oh ye of little faith. This guy may have known

about all the cameras on Imogene's townhouse. But he didn't know about the one I had installed at the apartment complex across the street."

I heard the unmistakable sound of his fingers flying over the keyboard once more. Within seconds, there was another video, this one with a direct view of Imogene's townhouse.

Including the driveway.

While it wasn't possible to get a clear view of what he was doing in the garage, it was obvious he dragged a body into the van. More importantly, the front license plate was in clear view.

"I'm texting you an address right now," he stated, then hesitated. "Unless you'd rather I call the police."

"I'm handling this myself," I said through gritted teeth. "There's too much at stake."

"I'll be on the next flight out. Promise me you won't do anything stupid before I get there."

"I can't make any promises," I answered darkly. "Not when it comes to her."

CHAPTER THIRTY

Imogene

I woke to darkness.

My head throbbed, my limbs heavy, as if weighed down by lead. My mouth was dry and parched, begging for even a drop of water. The air was stagnant, carrying the faint metallic tang of...what? Blood? Rust?

I blinked several times, trying to force my eyes to adjust to the black void around me.

Where am I?

My thoughts swirled, but all I could grasp were fragmented memories. Being at the townhouse. Packing. Taking out the garbage. Hearing a sound in the garage. Going inside to investigate and not finding anything.

Then the footsteps.

The arms around me.

The blinding pain in my head.

And then nothing.

What happened?

Did Liam find me? Was he the one who took me?

I struggled to push myself upright, my movements sluggish and disoriented. I touched a hand to my forehead, feeling something sticky. The floor beneath me was cold and rough against my bare feet, my shoes having been removed. At least I still had my clothes, but they did little to protect me against the chill that seeped into my skin.

Squinting in the darkness, I tried to make out any details in my surroundings. The space was small and cramped, the walls shrouded in shadow. There were no windows, only a faint, eerie glow coming from beneath the door.

I carefully reached out with my arms, searching for something familiar.

There was nothing. No furniture. No debris. Just emptiness.

The air was cooler near the far corner, a slight draft brushing against my skin. It was the only sensation to cling to, a whisper of the outside world.

What kind of place was this? A basement? It couldn't be. There weren't any basements in California. A storage room maybe? A warehouse? With no light or sound, it was impossible to know.

The air felt heavy, oppressive, like it was pressing down on me. A subtle smell lingered, sharp and acrid. It reminded me of bleach, but not clean — something that had tried and failed to mask something worse.

Trembling, I continued searching the space, my fingers grazing the wall. It was smooth but cold to the touch, like stone or concrete. I moved slowly, searching for anything — a light switch, a door, a clue.

Then my fingers caught on something.

Grooves.

I froze, my heart hammering as I traced the indentations with my fingertips. They were small but deep, carved into the wall. One. Two. Three. Four. Five. Then a space. Another cluster. And another.

Tally marks.

A chill raced down my spine as I kept moving, my hand following the lines etched into the surface. They went on and on, row after row. My breath hitched as I realized how many there were. Dozens. Maybe hundreds.

Someone had been keeping track of something.

Time, maybe?

I pulled my hand away, wiping my palm against my pants as if I could erase the sensation of those grooves from my skin. But the knowledge of them lingered, crawling beneath the surface.

Who had been here before me?

And where were they now?

The thought made my stomach churn, bile rising in my throat.

Then I heard it — quiet at first, like an echo in a long hallway.

Footsteps.

They grew steadily louder and closer with each passing second.

Pressing myself into the corner, I ran my hand along the wall again, searching frantically for something, *anything*, that could help me. A weapon. A crack to slip through. A hidden door.

There was nothing except the cold, unyielding wall at my back.

I squeezed my eyes shut, as if that would will the footsteps away. Would make me wake up from this nightmare.

But nothing would.

When they stopped outside my door, my entire body went rigid, every muscle pulled tight, as if that might somehow make me invisible. I bit my lip, willing myself not to make a sound, not even to breathe. My body trembled, and I wrapped my arms around myself, trying to stay still.

My ears strained to catch the faintest sound in the sudden silence, my heart beating so loudly I was sure whoever stood on the other side of the door could hear it.

Then a new sound cut through.

Metal clinking against metal.

It was faint but unmistakable, like keys being shifted in a pocket or held in a hand.

My stomach twisted.

The sound came again, louder this time, and I realized it wasn't just keys being moved. It was someone searching for the right one. Each jingle seemed to echo, magnified by the oppressive quiet of the room.

I pressed my back harder against the wall, my fingers splayed against the cold concrete, as if I could somehow push myself right through it. I held my breath, biting down on the inside of my cheek so hard I tasted blood.

Then came the click of a key being inserted into a lock.

It was slow and deliberate, as though whoever held it wasn't in any kind of rush. Like they knew they had all the time in the world.

The mechanism turned with a low, grinding noise, every rasp of metal against metal causing my stomach to tighten with dread.

I closed my eyes, trying to steady the wave of panic crashing through me. The smell of damp concrete and bleach grew sharper, mingling with the biting tang of fear that felt like it would suffocate me.

The door didn't open right away.

The lock had turned, but there was a pause. A heartbeat. Two. Three. Long enough for me to wonder if they were standing there, waiting, listening, just as I was.

The air in the room felt colder, heavier, like it was closing in on me. My palms were damp, and I curled my fingers into fists, my nails biting into my flesh in an effort to stay grounded.

And then the doorknob turned.

It moved slowly, the faint squeak piercing the silence like a scream.

Light spilled into the room, harsh and sudden. It burned against my eyes, forcing me to turn my head away as I squinted against the brightness. My heart was pounding so hard it felt like it might break free from my chest.

A shadow fell across the doorway, and I blinked rapidly, trying to make out the figure standing there.

But when it finally came into focus, my heart dropped at who my captor was.

CHAPTER THIRTY-ONE

Gideon

The tires screeched as I took another sharp turn, glancing at the GPS navigation in my SUV to see I still had a few more miles to go until I reached my destination. Every second felt like an eternity as my mind swirled with scenario after scenario about where Imogene could be.

"Lester Vargas," Henry's voice crackled over the car's speakers. "Former cop. Got booted for excessive force. Went into bounty hunting. It was the same story there. His license was revoked for repeated complaints of excessive force."

I tightened my grip on the steering wheel. That didn't bode well for Imogene. If he so much as hurt a single hair on her body, I'd make sure he regretted it for the rest of the short time he had left on earth.

"Connections?" I asked, swerving around slower cars on a street lined with shopping plazas and car dealerships.

"None that I could find," Henry replied. "But that doesn't mean there isn't one. Guys like Vargas don't exactly leave clean paper trails. If he's working for someone, it's probably a cash deal."

There was a pause before Henry spoke again, his concern evident.

"Look, I know you're not going to wait for me to land—"

"You'd be right," I interrupted.

"Just be careful. You're not bulletproof."

"Neither is he."

"This is just a job for him. You, on the other hand—"

"I'll be fine," I snapped, ending the call and focusing on navigating through intersection after intersection until finally pulling onto a narrow residential street.

The house wasn't hard to spot — a small, one-story structure tucked between other aging homes with the same van from the surveillance video parked out front. Except now, the rear license plate was back on.

I pulled my car down the block and killed the engine. Popping the glove box, I retrieved my weapon, checking the magazine and chamber with practiced efficiency before tucking it into my waistband. After scanning the street for any movement, I slipped out of the car and made my way toward the house.

The sun had set, casting everything in a shroud of darkness, the street lamps the only source of light. The neighborhood was a collection of forgotten dreams, houses in desperate need of a fresh coat of paint, fences sagging with the weight of neglect. It smelled like stale grease and overripe trash, a stench that clung to the air like a foul perfume.

I kept my head low, scanning for movement. Each step I took echoed, my shoes crunching over dirt and grime. A dog barked in the distance, its warning growl cut short by a command from its owner.

As I crossed the street toward Vargas' house, the weight of what I might find tightened my chest. The faint hum of an air conditioning unit buzzed in the background, nearly masking the distant murmur of a television. A gentle breeze blew around me, making a scrap of newspaper skitter across the concrete like a ghost.

The curtains in his house were drawn, but a flicker of light seeped through the cracks. My fingers brushed against the cool metal of my gun as I moved toward the side of the building, keeping to the shadows.

His house was no different from the others — a one-story box with peeling paint and a roof patched with mismatched shingles. The grass was yellowing, weeds sprouting through cracks in the concrete walkway leading to the front door. A faded lawn chair sat near the garage, its webbing frayed and sagging. The smell of cigar smoke lingered in the air, sharp and pungent.

Slipping through the broken gate and into the back yard, I surveyed my surroundings once more. It was in worse shape than the front. Scattered beer cans, a barbecue grill rusted beyond repair, and nothing but dust where grass once grew.

As I reached the edge of the house, I heard a creaking sound followed by footsteps. I froze, my hand instinctively tightening on the grip of my weapon as I carefully peered around the corner. Vargas stepped outside, his height and build matching the man in the surveillance video, a cigar clamped between his teeth.

As he leaned against the doorframe, he took a long drag from the cigar, the ember glowing red. He exhaled slowly, giving off an air of arrogance, as if he thought no one could touch him.

He was about to learn how wrong he was.

I waited until he turned his back before making my approach. The click of his lighter echoed as he reignited the cigar, oblivious to the predator closing in.

When I was close enough to see the shine of sweat on the back of his neck, I struck, grabbing him from behind and slamming him against the stucco siding.

His cigar tumbled to the ground as I twisted his arm

behind his back and shoved him inside. He cursed and tried to resist, but before he could make a move, I had him pinned against the wall, my gun pressed to the side of his head.

"Where is she?" I growled, my voice low and menacing.

"Who the hell—"

I slammed him harder against the surface, cutting off his words. "The girl you just took. Where is she?"

He grunted and struggled against my hold. "I don't know what you're talking about!"

I delivered a harsh blow to his sternum, leaving him gasping for air long enough to allow me to drag him to a nearby chair and secure him to it with zip ties. Every fiber of my being wanted to put a bullet in him right then and there, but he was my only lead as to where Imogene could be.

I needed him alive.

But the second I knew where she was, he would die.

And I would enjoy every minute of it.

As he tried to catch his breath, I scanned the messy living area. Takeout containers were stacked on the counter, beer bottles littered the table, and dirty dishes caked with food sat in the sink. But amidst the filth, there were expensive electronics. A high-end TV, multiple gaming consoles, a state-of-the-art sound system. Probably stolen.

"Let's try this again," I said once his wheezing stopped. "Where's the girl?"

"I told you. I don't know. I—"

Before he could utter another syllable, I pressed my gun to his knee and fired, using his own body to muffle the sound.

"All right!" he shouted, pain etched on his face as blood soaked the tile floor beneath him. "I was hired, okay?"

"By who?"

"No idea."

"Wrong answer." I grabbed a knife from the kitchen counter and thrust it into his open wound, eliciting another cry of agony.

"I swear! I'm telling you the truth. I don't know who it is."

"Then how did you get the job?"

"An unmarked package arrived on my doorstep one day. It was a burner phone." His eyes briefly darted toward a drawer in the kitchen before returning to me. "It rang, and the man said he could help me get back on the force if I did something for him. So I agreed."

I removed the knife from his bullet wound and approached the drawer, opening it to find a flip phone inside.

"Is this the burner?" I held it up.

Vargas hesitated, then nodded.

I opened it, wishing Henry was here. He'd be able to figure this thing out in a heartbeat. I hadn't operated a flip phone like this in ages. But I wasn't desperate enough to remove Vargas' restraints so he could do it for me.

Finally, I stumbled on the contacts, finding only one saved.

"Mom?" With a raised eyebrow, I clicked on the contact.

"What are you doing?" Vargas asked, clearly panicked.

I smirked, keeping my weapon trained on him. The metal glinted in the dim light of the room, a sharp contrast to the fear in his eyes.

"What do you think? Giving your mom a call."

"That's not how it works. I don't call him. He—"

I silenced him with a hush when the ringing cut off, a voice barking out, "This better be important."

"Where is she?" I demanded.

There was a pause. Then a low chuckle. "Well, well, well. If it isn't the man of the hour. I wondered when you'd show up."

"Tell me where she is, or I swear to God—"

"You'll what? Kill Vargas? Be my guest. I've got plenty more like him."

The indifference in his tone was infuriating. It almost made me not want to kill Vargas.

Almost.

But he was responsible for what happened to Imogene.

For that, he would pay.

"Where. Is. She?"

"She's an interesting subject, isn't she?" The man's tone turned contemplative, almost amused. "The daughter of a serial killer, yet so determined to be good. It's fascinating, really. I'm curious how much pressure it would take to break her. To see if she's truly her father's daughter."

My stomach churned, bile rising in my throat. "She's not."

"How can you be so sure? Haven't you ever wondered about the line between nature and nurture? Between good and evil? For instance, what turns someone like you, a man who once claimed to value life, into a killer? On the flip side, what makes a woman like Imogene, with that dark legacy of hers, cling so desperately to the illusion of innocence? I've always been curious about what drives human behavior. I've spent decades creating environments to test those limits. As you're well aware. After all, you spent nearly four years in several environments I created."

I blinked repeatedly, his words like a punch to the gut as the realization dawned on me.

"The fights..." I exhaled, the rage bubbling inside of me growing with every passing second. "That was you?"

"I prefer to call them experiments," he purred.

"You ruined my life," I growled. "And for what?"

"Ruined?" The man sounded genuinely perplexed. "I did no such thing. I gave you clarity. Stripped away the pretense, the delusions of morality, and showed you who you really are. Then I released you back into society as one last experiment. How would the killer I forged fare in the real world? Would you thrive? Or would you crumble under the weight of what you'd become?"

The room spun, and I gripped the edge of the table to steady myself as his words sunk in. All this time, I thought I was just a pawn in a twisted game for the wealthy elite's amusement. Instead, I was part of an experiment. What I thought was my escape wasn't an escape at all. It was planned.

Had this man been watching me all along?

"I killed because it was the only way to survive," I bit out harshly.

"Really? How much of your life lately has been about survival? How many of the lives you've taken since I released you have been about survival? Or have they been about something else?"

I didn't respond. I couldn't. Because not a single life I'd taken in the past year had been about survival. They were because of a hunger for blood, pure and simple.

"I planted the seed," the man continued, "but you watered it."

"I'm not that man anymore," I protested, but I could hear the doubt in my words.

"You've always been that man," he countered coolly. "I just gave you the appropriate environment in which to indulge your killer instincts."

I clenched and unclenched my fist, every word out of his mouth making me angrier and angrier. A part of me wondered if he was right. If I truly was a monster.

"But as you may or may not recall, I'm not an unreasonable man. I'm willing to make a deal."

"What kind of deal?" I asked hesitantly.

"You for her. Surrender yourself, and I'll let her go. No harm will come to her. You have my word."

A bitter laugh escaped my lips. "Your word doesn't mean shit."

"I guess you'll just have to take a leap of faith then."

Every instinct inside me screamed that this was a bad idea. To never trust this man who'd used and manipulated me in ways I couldn't even begin to fully wrap my head around.

But did I really have a choice?

I didn't see how. Worse, this asshole knew it. Knew Imogene was my weakness.

For years, I'd learned to show no weakness, as it could be used against me. I foolishly thought I was free, only for him to reappear and use my biggest weakness against me.

The bastard had planned everything. Every hellish fight, every scar, every sleepless night — he'd orchestrated it all. And now he had Imogene.

I needed to do everything I could to save her from the same fate I endured... Even if it meant sacrificing myself.

"Where?" I demanded.

The man chuckled softly. "That's the spirit. I'll send you the location. No tricks. No reinforcements. Come alone, or the deal is off. I could be wrong, but I doubt she'll last as long as you did in that cage."

The line went dead, leaving only the hollow echo of his words reverberating in my mind. A surge of rage overtook me and my vision blurred at the edges. I glared at Vargas, a pool of his blood staining the tile beneath him.

I erased the distance between us in two long strides and pressed my gun to his temple.

"Give me one reason," I growled, my face inches from his. "One reason I shouldn't decorate the wall with your brain right now."

"I swear, man!" Vargas cried, his voice cracking. "I didn't know he was this twisted. I just needed the money, man."

"So her life was worth...what? A couple of grand?"

"Five," he squeaked out.

"What's that?"

"What he paid me. Five grand."

I tightened the grip on my gun, my mind a blur of fury and grief. Then the man's voice echoed in my mind.

I planted the seed, but you watered it.

God, I wanted to kill this bastard. Wanted to pull the trigger and end this worthless excuse for a human being.

But that would only prove *him* right. Prove I truly was nothing more than a killer.

I refused to give him the satisfaction.

"You're not worth it," I muttered in disgust, lowering my gun, albeit reluctantly.

Vargas hung his head in relief, blowing out a long breath. "Thank you. Thank you, man."

"Don't thank me," I snapped as I turned toward the door. "You'll get what's coming to you."

Then I hurried out of the house, determined to save Imogene by any means necessary.

CHAPTER THIRTY-TWO

Imogene

The harsh light from the hallway sliced into the darkness of the room like a dagger. It should have been a welcome sight after the confusion of the past few minutes. But nothing could have prepared me for this, to be staring at the man who I thought was trying to help me. Keep me safe.

I should have known after his questions at the hospital he wasn't to be trusted. I convinced myself I was just overreacting.

But as I stared at the amused grin tugging on Agent Myers' lips, making him look nothing like the FBI agent I thought him to be, I knew I should have trusted my gut back then.

"Good evening, Ms. Prescott," Myers said, his voice as smooth as glass.

I pressed my back against the wall, my heart pounding so hard I felt it in my throat.

"How are you finding your accommodations?"

He adjusted his glasses with an air of casual arrogance. As if he was paying me a visit at my house. Not holding me captive in this dark, windowless room.

"What do you want?" I managed, my voice raw and trembling.

He tilted his head to the side. Then a slow smile spread across his face, the kind of smile you might give a child who asked a naïve question.

"What an excellent place to start."

He took another step closer, and I flinched before I could stop myself. He noticed, of course, and his grin only grew wider. As if he got off on my fear.

He probably did.

"The complexity of human nature has always intrigued me. What makes people tick? What pushes them to do the unthinkable? What breaks them?"

"I don't know what you're talking about," I retorted.

"You will soon enough."

He paced in front of me, his hands clasped behind his back.

"Your father was a fascinating case study. We studied serial killers extensively at the academy, but your father was unique. His ability to manipulate others into taking their own lives without pulling the trigger himself. It was almost...admirable. Was he shaped by his environment? Or was it simply...in his blood?" He stopped and turned to me, his sharp gaze piercing. "And that's where you come in."

"Me?" An icy chill ran down my spine.

"Of course. The daughter of a notorious killer, yet here you are...a caregiver. Or is it just an act? A mask you wear to convince the world, and yourself, that you're different?"

"I'm nothing like him." I tightened my hands into fists.

"How can you be sure?" His tone was eerily calm, but there was a glint of something in his eyes that made my stomach churn. "You've never been pushed to your limits. Never had to make the kind of choices that reveal who you truly are. That's why you're here. So we can find out together."

"You won't be finding out anything. I'm not playing your twisted games."

He chuckled softly, shaking his head like a teacher amused by a defiant student. "Oh, but you already are. You're not the first one, either. You see, I've spent years perfecting this. Creating environments where people reveal their true selves. Testing the limits of human nature."

He moved to the corner of the room, running his fingers along the tally marks etched into the wall.

"Do you know what these represent?" he asked, not looking at me. "Each mark signifies a choice, a moment when someone realized they were capable of crossing a line they never thought possible. Killing. Betraying. Surviving. It's astonishing, really."

"You're sick," I spat, swallowing down the bile in my throat.

He ignored my remark, turning back toward me with an almost fatherly smile. "This was once Samuel's cell."

My heart lurched at the mention of his name.

"And those marks... They represent each time he took a life."

I slowly shifted my gaze to the tally marks, seeing them in a completely new light now that I knew who made them. There were dozens, infinitely more than the lives my father took.

But he wasn't my father. This was different.

"And that was just when he was at this facility. There are even more at my other compounds."

"He didn't have a choice."

"Everyone has a choice," he countered with an expression of superiority. "I didn't even have to push that hard. He adapted so quickly, became exactly what he needed to be. A fighter. A survivor. A killer." His words hung in the air, echoing around me.

"And now," he continued, stepping closer, "I'm curious to see if the same potential lies in you. Will you rise above your father's legacy? Or will you embrace it?"

"You'll never find out," I snarled, glaring at him with all the defiance I could muster.

"We'll see," he taunted as he walked toward the door. "Everyone has their breaking point. Or perhaps I should say weakness. And I know exactly what yours is."

He leveled me with a sinister smile, leaving me speechless.

Then the door swung shut, plunging me back into darkness.

CHAPTER THIRTY-THREE

Gideon

The tires hummed against the asphalt as I drove toward the meeting point. The world outside my SUV felt strangely distant, the glow of streetlights casting long shadows on the empty road. My hands gripped the steering wheel so tight my knuckles ached, but I didn't ease up. I couldn't. Not when every second felt like it was ticking down to something I couldn't control.

I hit the call button on my cell, my throat tight as I waited for Henry to pick up. It rang twice before his voice came through.

"Tell me you have good news." His words were slightly muffled and distorted, no doubt due to the fact that he was currently on his airplane soaring across the country.

All for me.

"I wish I did," I said, my voice rough and strained. "All I know is he has Imogene."

"Who? Vargas?"

I shook my head even though he couldn't see me. "The same prick who took me."

"Wait. What? How do you know?"

"I just got off the phone with him. He called me an experiment, Henry. Said he wanted to see what it would take to turn me into a killer, and he did. He forced me to fight for my life, knowing exactly what it would do to me. And now, he's doing the same thing to Imogene. He's going to push her, test her."

"Jesus Christ," Henry muttered, taking a moment to process this. Then he became the analytical man I always knew him to be. "What can you remember about his appearance? Anything at all?"

"I told you when I first showed up on your doorstep. He never revealed his face. He always stayed in the shadows."

"What do you need me to do?"

"I need you to do whatever you can to figure out where he's keeping Imogene. Call Melanie's dad. He offered to help me take down Liam. No doubt he'll help with this, too. You should probably reach out to

Imogene's parents, as well. Let them know what's going on."

"I should be landing in a little more than an hour. I can—"

"I won't be here," I blurted out before I could stop the words.

"What do you mean?" he asked hesitantly, as if already sensing where this conversation was headed.

"I offered him a trade. Or, more accurately, *he* offered *me* a trade. Me for Imogene."

"You realize it's most likely a trap, right?"

"Of course it's a trap. But until you figure out where Imogene is, this is the best option I have. If I go to him, I can buy us more time."

"Time for what?"

"Time for her to stay alive. Time for you to figure out where the hell she is," I snapped, my frustration boiling over. I forced myself to take a breath, loosening my grip on the wheel. "Just...time, Henry."

He was silent for a moment, and I could hear the sound of him typing furiously at his laptop, probably in the hopes of finding something that might stop me from going down this path. But nothing would. This was my only option right now. My only way to get to Imogene.

"I'm supposed to go to an address up in Tustin. I checked it out. It's just some commuter lot off the free-way. I'm guessing my ride will be waiting there. I have no idea what will happen once I go with them, but I need you to do me a favor."

"What's that?"

"Get Imogene out safe. And make sure she's taken care of if I don't—"

"Don't talk like that," he interjected quickly. "You're getting her back. Both of you are walking away from this."

A bitter laugh fell from my throat. "You don't know that."

"Neither do you," he shot back.

The corner of my mouth twitched at that. Classic Henry, always ready to argue with me when I needed it most. Or give me a dose of reality.

"Please, Henry," I begged, my voice catching. "If I don't make it, I need you to promise you'll get her out. That you'll do whatever it takes."

There was a long silence on the other end. Finally, Henry exhaled, a heavy sound that carried the weight of a lifetime of friendship.

"I promise," he said.

"Thank you. For everything. For always having my back, even when I didn't deserve it. You've always been the one person I could depend on, and I just want you to know how much that means—"

"We're not doing this, Sam. If you want to revisit this discussion in forty years when we're both bickering like two old men about who caught the biggest fish, we will, but we're not doing it now. Not today."

"Henry…"

"No," he cut me off, his voice stronger now. "We're not saying goodbye. Not yet."

I smiled faintly, even though my chest felt like it was caving in. "I'll see you soon, then."

"Damn right you will," he said firmly, although I could hear the emotion clogging his throat. Then, after a beat, he added, "Brothers for life, Sam."

"Brothers for life," I responded, unsure what else to add.

There was so much more I wanted to tell him, but I knew he'd berate me yet again. Instead, I ended our conversation there, hoping it wasn't the last time I'd ever speak to him.

The remainder of the drive up to Tustin went by quicker than I anticipated, the traffic unusually light. Before I knew it, I was pulling off the freeway and into the nearby carpool lot, a wide expanse of cracked asphalt littered with cigarettes and discarded fast-food wrappers. A single overhead light flickered in the middle, casting long, wavering shadows over the faded lines.

I pulled into a spot near the edge of the lot, cutting the engine and plunging myself into silence. The quiet was deafening, the kind that made every little noise feel amplified.

Minutes ticked by, each one slower than the last. The darkness outside seemed to press in closer, and my mind raced with every possible scenario about what I was about to face.

Then again, I knew precisely what I was about to face. I'd been here before.

When I first escaped, I swore I'd never do anything to put myself in this position again. That I'd rather die than return to that hell.

That was before Imogene.

I'd do anything to save her.

Even if it meant enduring an eternity of torture.

A train horn blew in the distance just as headlights pierced the darkness, their glare reflecting off my mirrors. My pulse kicked up when a black van rolled into the lot, stopping a few spaces away, its windows tinted so dark I couldn't see inside.

I shot off a quick text to Henry with the plate number, then shoved my phone into the glove box. Steeling myself for the uncertainty of what was to come, I slid out of my car and approached the van, each step measured, deliberate. The driver's door opened, and a burly man climbed out, his massive frame silhouetted against the headlights. He was built like a tank, his movements precise as he turned to face me.

"Arms out and legs wide," he barked, his voice low and gravelly.

I complied as he stepped forward, his hands rough and methodical as they swept over my arms, chest, and legs. When he was satisfied I wasn't armed or wired, he bound my wrists behind my back with a pair of zip ties, then opened the back of the van, the sight of it reminding me of my years spent in captivity.

"Get in."

With a nod, I walked forward, climbing inside.

He approached, pulling a hood out of the back of his jeans. The sight of it caused bile to rise in my throat. Memories of other hoods, other times, flashed through my mind, but I forced them down, taking a deep breath. Then he yanked the hood over my head, plunging me into an even deeper darkness.

"Remember the deal. No funny business or the girl dies."

I nodded just as the doors slammed close behind me.

After a few moments, the van started moving, the hum of the engine vibrating through the floorboard. I focused on the turns, counting them in my head — left, right, another left — trying to keep track of where we were going. But the driver wasn't stupid. After a while, the pattern changed, the car taking random turns, doubling back, speeding up and slowing down until I lost all sense of direction.

The hood was stifling, the fabric pressing against my face. I tried to steady my breathing, forcing myself to focus. This wasn't the first time I'd been in a situation like this. This was how we were always transported, with hoods on our heads, making it impossible to know where we were.

After several hours of driving, the van slowed, the tires crunching over gravel as it drove over a long unpaved road. Finally, the van stopped. The back door opened, and rough hands grabbed me, hauling me out.

"Move," the man growled, shoving me forward.

I stumbled but caught myself, the ground uneven beneath my shoes. The air was different here, sharp with the scent of manure and damp earth.

I tried to make out my surroundings, but the hood was too thick. All I could do was listen, every sound amplified in the darkness. A distant creak, like rusted hinges. Footsteps on gravel. Then we were inside a building, the air thicker with the stench of blood and death.

It sent a chill down my spine, the smell bringing forward memories of the years I spent in captivity.

Another rough shove sent me stumbling into what felt like a small, enclosed space. After my zip ties were replaced with shackles, the hood was ripped off. I blinked against the sudden brightness, my eyes struggling to adjust.

When they did, the first thing I saw was the cell. Bare walls without a single piece of furniture.

The second thing I saw was him.

Agent Myers stood in the doorway, his expression calm and almost amused as he watched me.

"Welcome back, 671," he said, his voice as smooth and polished as ever, referring to me with the number that was once tattooed on my arm.

My stomach churned, but I forced myself to hold his gaze, masking any hint of surprise or confusion from seeing him here.

His smile widened, a chilling expression that didn't reach his eyes. "I've been looking forward to this."

CHAPTER THIRTY-FOUR

Gideon

"I'm here now," I ground out, glaring at Myers with pure disgust in my eyes. Just me, him, and the icy floor beneath my knees. "Let Imogene go."

Myers chuckled, the sound low and condescending. He clasped his hands behind his back, pacing a slow circle around me. His dark suit was spotless, his tie perfectly knotted, an unsettling contrast to the cold, grimy concrete walls surrounding us.

"Ah, yes, our bargain. I did say I'd release her once you came, didn't I?"

"You didn't just say it. You promised it. Let her go."

Myers came to a stop in front of me and tilted his head to the side, studying me with dark, calculating eyes. "Circumstances have changed."

A muscle in my jaw twitched, but I forced myself to hold his gaze. "Circumstances haven't changed. I'm here. You don't need her anymore."

"Oh, but that's where you're wrong." Myers' tone took on that detached, clinical edge that made my skin crawl.

From the second he showed up at the house to ask Imogene about the break-in, I sensed there was something off about him. Sensed I shouldn't have trusted him. Now I knew why.

But if he already knew who I was, why all the questions? Or was it just another test? Another twisted game?

I had a feeling I already knew the answer.

"Imogene is proving to be far more fascinating than I anticipated," he continued. "Do you know how rare it is to find someone with her background, her resilience, her...potential?"

"Potential?" I pushed down the bile rising in my throat at hearing him talk about her like she was just another test subject.

Then again, that was all any of us were to him. Just pawns in his game of power and control.

"She's quite fascinating. In fact, it was her father that prompted me to study criminology in college. To eventually join the Bureau in the hopes of profiling criminals just like him. Figure out what makes them tick. And

Imogene's father, Domenic Jaskulski, he wasn't just your run-of-the-mill serial killer."

A twisted grin curled on his face that churned my stomach.

Almost like he respected Imogene's father.

"What I loved about him was the game he played. How he studied his targets for months before determining if they were what he was looking for. He knew exactly what to do in order to manipulate them into doing precisely what he wanted, which ended with them taking their own lives. It's quite remarkable if you think about it — a serial killer who never actually killed. Well, until later on," he added quickly.

"Imogene's nothing like him," I hissed, pinning him with a lethal glare.

"You see, that's where we disagree. I think the more accurate statement would be that she *pretends* she's not like him. Deep down, she's more like her father than she wants to believe."

"What do you want from her? From me? From all of this?"

"Answers. Her father's actions made me think. If he was able to manipulate people into taking their own lives, it stood to reason one would be able to manipulate someone into killing other people."

"You're insane." I lunged for him, but the chains

attached to my wrists and ankles prevented me from reaching him.

Instead, he stared at me with that same smug look on his face.

"Am I? Or am I simply asking the questions everyone else is too afraid to confront?" Myers' voice rose slightly, his eyes gleaming with a fervor that bordered on madness. "What creates a killer? Nature? Nurture? Circumstance? Something else entirely? It's a fascinating subject. One I'm looking forward to exploring with Imogene."

"You're wasting your time," I snapped. "Imogene's smarter than that. She's *stronger* than that. She won't let you manipulate her into becoming something she's not. And she's not like..." I trailed off.

"Like what?" He smirked, a knowing gleam in his eyes. "Finish your thought. She's not like...what?"

"Me," I answered. "She's not like me. Or her father. Or you."

"I guess we'll just have to see who's right. Won't we?"

I glared at him, my chest heaving. Every instinct screamed at me to lash out, to fight, to rip that smug look off his face. But that's exactly what he wanted. I wouldn't give him the satisfaction.

Myers took a step back. "Get some rest. You're going to need it. The real fun begins soon. I can't wait for you to see the surprise I have in store for you. I truly believe I've outdone myself."

The door clanged shut behind him, leaving me alone in the suffocating silence of the cell. The walls felt closer now, the air heavier. But my resolve hardened.

I wouldn't let him win. Not this time.

Not with Imogene's life at stake.

CHAPTER THIRTY-FIVE

Imogene

The zip ties cut into my wrists like sharp claws as a guard dragged me down the hallway, my pulse pounding louder with every step. The stale, musty air clung to my skin like a second layer. Every breath I took tasted metallic, as though the walls themselves were turning to rust around me.

The men surrounding me didn't speak, their heavy boots pounding in rhythm with my erratic heartbeat. I strained to focus on anything else — counting the flickering overhead lights, noting the chipped paint on the walls — but nothing could drown out the knot twisting tighter in my stomach.

They may not have told me where they were taking me, but I already knew. And when we turned the corner and I saw the metal structure looming ahead, my knees buckled, all the air whooshing out of my lungs.

I'd heard Gideon's stories. Over the past few days, I was even forced to watch videos of his fights that Myers kept like a prized home movie collection.

But nothing could have prepared me to see that cage in person.

It stood in the center of a large, dimly lit room, its metal walls stained with streaks of rust. Or blood. I couldn't tell which. The bars looked thick and unforgiving, dull in places and sharpened to jagged edges in others, as though years of violence had reshaped them.

A foul stench rolled over me. Sweat, blood, and something acrid curdled in the back of my throat. I gagged, turning my face away, but the smell followed.

My ears buzzed with phantom sounds — fists hitting flesh, bones snapping, screams that wouldn't stop. None of it was real, not right now, but I could still hear them echoing in my head, leaving me frozen in place.

"Move."

The guard shoved me forward, and I stumbled, my bare feet scraping against the cold, gritty floor. The cage seemed to grow larger with each step, its oppressive presence swallowing me whole.

They forced me into a chair mere inches away from the cage, the metal biting through my thin clothes. On either side of me, the guards stood motionless, their eyes fixed ahead. I didn't dare look at them. My gaze was glued to the structure in front of me.

A pit.

A stage.

A tomb.

For a moment, I couldn't breathe. The fear clawing at my chest wasn't new. It had been with me since the moment I woke up in my cell, however long ago that was.

But now it felt sharper, deeper. Like it had taken root in my very bones.

"Quite the sight, isn't it?" Myers' voice slithered through the haze of my thoughts, making me flinch.

I hadn't even noticed him step into the room. He stood a few feet away, his hands tucked casually into his pockets, his face a picture of smug satisfaction.

I didn't answer. I couldn't. My throat was raw, my response stolen by the weight of what I knew was about to happen. What I was about to witness.

He leaned closer, his voice dropping to a conspiratorial whisper. "It's amazing what a couple dozen metal bars and a lock will do to a person."

I turned my head away, but he didn't stop.

"It strips them down to their most primal instincts, separating the weak from the strong. Survival, Ms. Prescott. That's all that matters in there. You'll see for yourself soon enough."

I wanted to scream at him, tell him I wasn't afraid of

him, that I'd survived worse. But the words died on my tongue. All I could do was sit there, frozen, as the door at the far end of the room creaked open, revealing an endless void.

I said a silent prayer, hoping it wasn't Gideon who would appear from the darkness.

I should have known I wouldn't get my wish.

He emerged slowly, a dark silhouette moving closer. My chest tightened, my body instinctively leaning forward, despite my restraints. As if I could somehow reach him, pull him back, shield him from this nightmare.

When he stepped fully into the light, the world around me seemed to tilt. It took everything in me not to wail at the sight of him, his feet bare, dress pants torn, his scars on full display. I wanted to call his name, but the sound wouldn't come. My throat felt like it was closing, my breath hitching in shallow gasps as tears blurred my vision.

And when his eyes fell on me, his nostrils flared, a hint of that rage I'd seen in all those videos shining through.

He strained against the bindings, his muscles taut as he fought to get closer. "Imogene."

It was barely more than a rasp, a sound torn from his throat like it physically hurt to say my name.

The despair in his voice unraveled me completely.

Tears spilled freely down my cheeks, hot and unrelenting. I wanted to throw myself at him. Take his place. Protect him the way he'd always fought to protect me. But I couldn't move. The guards held me in place, their presence a cold reminder of my helplessness.

"You shouldn't be here," I choked out, my voice cracking under the weight of the words.

"I'll always come for you. It'll be okay. We'll be okay."

I shook my head, unable to speak, my chest heaving as a sob caught in my throat. I didn't see how we would be okay. How we'd get out of this.

Myers' laugh cut through the moment, sharp and cruel. "How romantic. Now if you two love birds are done, it's time for your surprise." He turned his attention toward Gideon, a sadistic smile curling his lips. "Consider it a gift. After the hours of enjoyment you've provided me, it was the least I could do for you."

He nodded toward one of the guards, who retreated down the same hallway Gideon had just come from. Tense anticipation filled the room as we waited to see what Myers' surprise would be. I knew it wouldn't be good.

I just didn't realize how depraved it would actually be.

CHAPTER THIRTY-SIX

Gideon

"What are you talking about?" I seethed, glaring at Myers as he approached.

The air in the room was stifling, thick with sweat and anticipation as I stood in this cage once more. It was the last place I wanted to be, but I found some comfort that Imogene was still alive. I hated that she was here, hated that Myers had dragged her into my nightmare, forcing her to see parts of me I never wanted her to know.

Parts I'd hoped to bury.

I should have known better.

"Oh, you're going to love it," Myers replied, the amusement in his tone making my skin crawl.

A heavy silence fell over the room, and my gaze

floated toward the corridor as a shadow moved in the distance, distorted by the dim lighting.

Then I heard footsteps, uneven and hesitant. They weren't charging in like some confident fighter eager to prove their worth. These steps were reluctant, as if being forced.

I knew they were.

A figure emerged slowly, barely distinguishable at first. Broad shoulders. Tall. Male. Something about the shape tugged at the edges of my memory, but the dim lighting played tricks on my eyes.

As the man stepped into the light, his features became clearer. Gaunt, hollowed cheeks. Face hidden with an overgrown beard. Hair disheveled and damp with sweat. Clothes hanging off him like they no longer fit, although they once did.

But when I peered into his eyes, the realization hit me, the breath whooshing out of my lungs.

Liam.

He looked like a ghost of himself — pale, trembling, his eyes darting around the room like a trapped animal. For a second, I thought I might be hallucinating. But it was him. The man who'd betrayed me. The man who'd wanted me dead.

The man I'd sworn to destroy.

I should have known Myers would do something like this. Hell, he'd probably had Liam for months. Probably knew where he was all along. Hell, *he* probably planted those photos at Imogene's house and staged the break-in for some reason I couldn't even begin to fathom. Was he responsible for what happened to Ollie, too?

I wanted to kick myself for not realizing it all sooner. I'd been so intent on blaming Liam that I refused to consider it could be anyone else.

Now I feared Imogene would pay for my mistake.

We all would.

Liam's gaze locked onto mine, and the terror within was unmistakable. He knew where he was and what was expected of him.

He took another shaky step forward, his movements jerky, as though his legs were on autopilot while his mind screamed at him to run.

I'd imagined this moment a thousand times — his face bloodied, his body broken, his cries for mercy falling on deaf ears. I'd dreamed of it, planned for it, savored the thought of making him feel even a fraction of what I'd endured because of him.

Now here he was, trembling, vulnerable, and looking at me like I held his life in his hands.

But this?

This wasn't the Liam I'd envisioned.

This wasn't the smug, self-assured bastard who'd laughed with me over beers while secretly planning to kill me.

This was a broken man.

"Surprise," Myers drawled, his grin widening. "You wanted revenge, didn't you? Well, I'm giving it to you. On a silver platter."

Liam's eyes darted to the cage, then back at me, panic bleeding into his expression.

The guard shoved him inside and he fell to his knees, only to be yanked back up. Meeting my gaze, his lips moved silently, forming a word or maybe a plea, but no sound came out.

As I watched him, a feeling I never expected washed over me.

Pity.

It burned in my chest, a reminder of the man I used to be. The man who believed in fairness, in justice, in humanity.

Before my business partner left me for dead.

And yet, as I looked at Liam, trembling and terrified, I couldn't help but see a reflection of the man I was when I was thrown into this cage for the first time. The fear. The desperation. The crushing realization that there was only one way to survive.

I didn't want to feel this. Didn't want to see myself in him.

"This is what you've been waiting for, isn't it?" Myers said, circling the cage like a predator. "Poetic justice. You, the avenging angel. Him, the traitor who wanted you dead. And her..." He nodded toward Imogene, who was staring at us, wide-eyed and silent. "The woman who started it all."

My hands balled into fists, jaw clenched. I didn't want to play his sick game anymore. I didn't want to be his puppet, dancing to the tune of his twisted fantasies.

But what choice did I have?

"The rules are simple," Myers said, his voice slicing through my thoughts like a death knell. "There are no rules. The match ends when one of you is dead."

A choked sob echoed in the room, and I pulled my attention away from Liam, meeting Imogene's tear-stained eyes.

"Whatever he says, whatever he does, don't listen to him," I told her urgently. "Do you hear me, Imogene? Stay strong. Don't let him break you. Promise me."

She opened her mouth, more confused than anything. But she must have picked up on my desperation.

With her lower lip trembling, she nodded. "I promise."

Myers clapped his hands, his tone mockingly cheerful. "Enough stalling. Let's get this show started."

The lights above the cage flickered to life, bathing the room in a harsh, clinical glow. The guards approached Liam first to undo his restraints before moving to me, more guards keeping their weapons trained on us to make sure we didn't attack anyone we weren't supposed to.

"Whatever happens next," I continued, keeping my voice steady. "Close your eyes, Imogene. Don't watch. Don't let him win by making you a part of this."

She shook her head, a tiny but defiant movement. "I'm not going to do that. I promised to stay by your side even during your darkest moments. This is one of them. No matter what happens, know that I'm with you. That I love you."

"I love you, too," I told her, not wanting to look away for fear it might be one of the last times I'd ever see her.

Even when the bell cut through, signaling the start of the match, I couldn't bring myself to turn around. To say goodbye to Imogene.

It wasn't until her expression twisted into one of absolute horror that I whirled around, meeting Liam's wild eyes as he rushed toward me, a knife clutched tightly in his hand.

CHAPTER THIRTY-SEVEN

Imogene

I didn't want to watch. This was too much. Too horrific.

Too depraved.

But I refused to let Gideon endure this alone.

So I looked on in revulsion as Liam stormed toward him, his body coiled like a predator, his movements erratic and wild. His eyes were alight with something feral, a crazed madness that chilled me to the bone. He wasn't Liam anymore. He was a creature driven by desperation, survival, and the sick thrill of bloodlust.

With a guttural roar, Liam swung his blade clumsily but with terrifying force, aiming for Gideon's chest. I held my breath, the seconds stretching into an eternity as Gideon deftly sidestepped the blow with fluid, instinctual movements. Relief surged through me for a fleeting moment...until he made no move to retaliate.

Why wasn't he fighting back?

Liam snarled, baring his teeth like an animal as he swiped again, his strikes fast and frenzied. Gideon continued to dodge each attack with grace and precision, but not without consequence. The blade grazed his forearm, a crimson line blooming against his skin.

I flinched, a strangled gasp escaping my throat as though I'd been struck myself. I dug my nails into my palms, the sting grounding me in the midst of the chaos.

The room seemed to shrink around me, the cage's chain-link walls blurring at the edges of my vision. The sickening scrape of boots on the concrete floor and the sharp clang of the blade against metal echoed in my ears, amplifying the pounding of my heartbeat.

"It's remarkable, isn't it," Myers' voice slithered into my ear, soft and mocking.

I didn't look at him. I couldn't. My eyes remained locked on Gideon, silently pleading with him.

Go on the offensive. Fight back. Do something.

Myers leaned closer, the faint scent of his aftershave churning my stomach. "He's fighting against his natural instinct to kill... All for you."

His words pierced through me like a knife, twisting and cruel.

"You should have seen him in his prime," Myers

continued, his tone dripping with smugness. "The way he practically disemboweled his opponents — it was art. No hesitation. No mercy. Just brutal efficiency. But now... He hesitates."

"You're disgusting," I hissed. "These are real people. Real lives."

"I know," Myers said, his wicked grin spreading. His eyes gleamed with a twisted delight as he gestured toward the cage. "That's what makes it so interesting. To see how people react when it's life or death. I thought Liam would cower first, but look at him. Thriving. All because of that cage."

Liam lunged again, this time feinting left before driving his knife into Gideon's side. The blade missed its mark, but it still raked across his ribs, leaving a trail of blood just above his tattoo.

"No," I whispered.

Gideon staggered but didn't falter. His hands remained empty, his feet steady as he danced around Liam's frenzied movements. He wasn't fighting. He was enduring.

Liam was nothing but an animal now, rabid and cruel, driven by instincts that had long since overtaken reason. His chest heaved as he slashed and swung with reckless abandon, his grip on the knife white-knuckled. Spittle flew from his mouth as he let out a guttural yell, his face twisted in a grotesque mask of rage and desperation. His movements lacked any precision, but it didn't matter. He was relentless.

I bit down hard on my lip, trying to block out the sounds — the sharp intake of Gideon's breath, the sickening crunch of a fist connecting with flesh, Myers' vile amusement. But I couldn't.

I wanted to scream at Liam. At Myers. At the guards standing motionless by the exits. But most of all, I wanted to scream at Gideon to stop being so noble. Stop holding back. Just fight.

I had a feeling he wouldn't out of principle, even if it cost him his life.

Another blow sent Gideon staggering, and he fell to his knees, his breath ragged as blood dripped steadily from his wounds. Liam hovered above him, the blade poised for the final strike, a wild animal ready to kill to save himself.

And that was precisely what he was.

Myers had remarked that the cage changed people.

I'd just witnessed it first-hand.

"Enough!" I screamed, the word ripping from me with a primal force. "I'll do whatever you want, just stop this!"

Myers gave one of the guards a signal, and he approached the cage, sticking a long pole inside and zapping Liam, forcing him to his knees with a painful jolt of electricity.

"No, Imogene," Gideon managed to say, his voice a broken rasp as he lifted his gaze toward me. His face was scrunched in determination, his eyes burning with his plea. "Don't."

I shook my head, tears streaming down my cheeks. "I can't... I can't watch you die." My voice cracked, and I felt my resolve shatter.

Myers' laughter cut through. "How touching."

He yanked me to my feet and pushed me toward the cage. A guard opened the door and Myers dragged me inside.

Was he going to make *me* fight Liam in Gideon's place? Or something else? Something much more depraved?

With a sinister grin, Myers moved toward Liam and snatched the knife out of his hands. He used it to cut the zip ties from my wrists before forcing me to take it.

"Kill him." He nodded at Liam.

"What?" I asked, unable to mask my surprise. "I can't—"

"Rules are rules, Ms. Prescott. The match doesn't end until one of the fighters is dead. You want to end it? You need to kill one of them."

"Don't do it," Gideon whispered. "You're better than this. Better than me."

"Remember what Liam did," Myers taunted. "He shot the man you loved, then paid someone to cover it up.

He manipulated you into inviting him into your bed, between your legs, when all along he was the one who wanted him dead. All so he could have you to himself. It was never about money to him. It was always about *you*. He tried to kill the man you loved. And you're going to let him get away with it?"

I looked between Gideon and Liam, my insides twisted up. "I... I can't..."

"You can," Myers urged, his voice low and hypnotic. "You've imagined it, haven't you? What it would feel like to have that kind of power. To be the one in control. To make someone pay. To make *him* pay. An eye for an eye, Ms. Prescott. He deserves this."

"No one deserves this."

"Oh, come on," he sneered. "You've spent your whole life pretending to be good. Pretending you're not your father's daughter. But deep down, you know the truth. You're just like him."

"Imogene, look at me." Gideon's voice cut through the fog in my head. "You are not him. You're good. You're strong. You don't have to do this."

My hands shook. My heart pounded. Myers' voice dripped into my ears, smooth and venomous. "He's lying to you. He knows you want this. He's just afraid you'll realize it's true."

I clutched the blade tighter in my hand, as if it were the only thing keeping me grounded. My vision blurred, my breaths coming in ragged gasps. Gideon begged me to stop. Myers taunted me to act. If I did what he wanted, he'd win. But if I refused, he'd win, too.

It was an impossible choice.

I once read something about the difference between a hero and a villain. How a hero wasn't inherently good, and a villain wasn't inherently evil. Instead, the difference was in the sacrifice each was willing to make. A hero would sacrifice those he loved to save the world. But a villain... A villain would sacrifice everyone else to save those he loved.

Maybe Myers was right.

Maybe I *was* a villain.

I spun on my heels, my sudden motion catching Myers by surprise.

I leveled him with a stare, my mouth curling up in the corners.

"I am *not* my father," I declared, my voice trembling but resolute.

Then I drove the blade into his stomach.

CHAPTER THIRTY-EIGHT

Gideon

Everything felt suspended in time, each second stretching painfully as I struggled to wrap my head around what just happened.

My vision blurred from the loss of blood, but I forced myself to focus. Myers lay crumpled on the ground, his eyes wide with shock as he futilely tried to stop the bleeding from the deep gash across his abdomen. The pool of blood beneath him widened, the vivid crimson stark against the cold concrete floor.

Imogene stood over him, the blade still clenched in her trembling hand, her gaze fixed on Myers. Her breaths came in short, sharp gasps, her chest heaving as though she couldn't draw enough air.

As though she couldn't comprehend what she'd done.

"Imogene," I choked out, my voice raspy and raw, but I didn't have time to get to her.

A percussive shot tore through the space, forcing my eyes from hers. I whirled toward the source, the guards charging toward us like a pack of wolves descending on their prey.

I didn't think. I just moved, the adrenaline surging through me like fire. My muscles burned, protesting every step, but I didn't care. I was focused on one thing only — keeping Imogene safe.

"Liam!" I barked, my voice sharp enough to cut through the noise. He jerked his head toward me.

He was wild-eyed, panting, his hands red with blood. *My* blood.

He looked less like a man and more like an animal.

"They'll kill us all if we don't work together," I instructed, each word measured and deliberate. "Do you understand? We have to fight them together."

I never thought I'd willingly work with Liam again. Not after what he did to me. Not after he stole years of my life and tried to take everything I cared about.

But now, survival trumped revenge.

His eyes darted to the approaching guards, then back to me. For a heartbeat, I feared he'd use this opportunity to let me die, to finish what he started years ago.

Then he gave a sharp nod, his eyes gleaming with a primal determination.

The first guard reached the cage, his gun raised. I surged forward, driving my fist into his jaw, the crack reverberating through my knuckles. He went down hard, and I grabbed his gun.

Behind me, Liam let out a guttural growl as he picked up the knife Imogene had dropped, the blade catching the light as he ran out of the cage, driving it into another guard's stomach. The man screamed, crumpling to the ground, but Liam didn't stop. He moved like a rabid beast, his strikes wild and uncoordinated but devastatingly effective, eliminating guard after guard.

I hated that I needed him. Hated that I was relying on the same man who had betrayed me, who had taken everything from me. But in this moment, I couldn't afford to hate him.

I moved purely on instinct, the muscle memory from years of fighting kicking in. Every breath felt like fire, every step like dragging my limbs through molasses, but I didn't stop. I couldn't.

Not with Imogene's life at stake.

She was frozen in the corner of the cage, her wide, tear-filled eyes darting between me and the guards. One of them lunged toward her, and I fired the gun without hesitation. The bullet hit its mark, sending him stumbling back.

The air reeked of sweat, blood, and gunpowder. Every movement sent fresh waves of pain through my battered body, but I kept going.

Another guard rushed me, larger and faster than the others. I barely managed to sidestep him, but he knocked the gun from my hand before grabbing my injured arm, twisting it until I heard a sickening pop. I screamed in agony, dropping to one knee. Thankfully, it was right in front of the knife I'd refused to use during my fight.

I wrapped my fingers around it and slashed upward. The guard fell, clutching his throat.

My breaths came in ragged gasps. Blood dripped from my side, my arm hung limp, but I couldn't stop. I had to make sure Imogene made it out of here alive... Even if I didn't.

I became the man Meyers turned me into. A ruthless killing machine who took lives without a single care. When one guard dropped, another would take his place, who I'd kill without mercy.

The chaos around me was deafening, but I couldn't hear any of it. I was in a trance.

But with each guard I took out, I felt myself getting weaker and weaker, my motions growing slower.

"Gideon! Behind you!" Imogene's voice cut through as I took a moment to gather some strength.

I stumbled around, time standing still as I stared down the barrel of a gun.

I told my body to move, but I was too slow to react after the beating I'd taken.

Then I felt something slam into me, pushing me to the floor at the same moment as the shot rang out.

Time seemed to stop as I tried to make sense out of what happened. But then I saw Imogene.

She was inches away, where I was standing seconds ago, her face contorted in shock and pain. She took a step back, then another. Then she collapsed, blood staining her shirt.

Rage filled me, pulling me to my feet, and I rushed the guard, snapping his neck in one swift motion and tossing him aside like a rag doll.

I scrambled toward Imogene, pressing my hands to the wound on her stomach, desperate to stop the flow of blood.

"It'll be okay. You'll be okay," I managed to say through the tightness in my throat, peppering kisses to her face.

The frenzy around us grew louder — the sound of gunfire, shouting, and heavy boots pounding against the floor. I snapped my attention away for a split second. The remaining guards fell one by one, taken out by men in tactical gear storming the compound.

At first, I was confused, but when I saw Henry and Alexander pull up the rear, I was momentarily relieved, sending up a silent prayer that my friend finally came through.

But any relief was fleeting as I looked back at Imogene, her skin pale and her breathing shallow.

"I... I'm so sorry," she strained to say, her voice barely a whisper, fragile and broken.

"Don't," I choked out, cradling her closer to me as if holding her tighter could somehow keep her with me. "You have nothing to be sorry for."

Tears burned at the corners of my eyes, but I refused to let them fall. Not now. Not when she needed me to be strong.

"I never should have pushed you away," she gasped, each breath becoming more difficult than the last. "Never should have run from you. Never should have wasted time."

"You didn't," I said fiercely, grabbing her trembling hand tightly in mine.

My gaze fell to the ring on her finger, the blood-stained diamond a brutal reminder of everything we'd fought for — and everything we stood to lose. My chest ached, a raw, relentless pressure that made it hard to breathe. But I couldn't let her see.

"And now," I continued, forcing a steadiness into my voice I didn't feel, "we'll have all the time in the world together. I promise." I pressed a trembling kiss to her forehead, my lips lingering against her skin. "We're free."

A faint, almost imperceptible laugh escaped her lips. "I didn't take you for an optimist," she murmured, the sound so feeble it shattered something deep inside me.

I tilted my head back, blinking rapidly against the tears threatening to spill. "I'm not," I whispered, my voice shaking. "I'm a realist. And you *will* make it out of here. You hear me? You do *not* get to die in this goddamn cage." I pressed my forehead to hers, desperate to anchor us both. "Just stay with me, Imogene. Please. You can't leave me."

"Gideon," a voice worked its way through the haze, followed by a firm hand on my shoulder.

I jerked my head up, blinking through the tears to see Henry standing over me, his face tight with urgency. Behind him, medics surged forward, pushing a stretcher, medical bags slung on their shoulders.

"Let go of her," Henry said, his voice calm but firm.

His words didn't register. I stared at him, trying to comprehend, but the meaning slipped through my fingers like sand. Let go of her? How could I?

"Please, Gideon," he begged, the faintest crack of emotion breaking through. "Every second counts. There's a med-evac helicopter waiting outside, but you have to let her go."

I looked back down at Imogene, her face ashen, her breaths shallow. The blood pooling beneath her seemed brighter than before, its sickening vibrancy clawing at my chest.

"I can't," I rasped, shaking my head, my fingers tightening around hers. "I need her."

"You're not losing her," Henry said, crouching beside me. "But you have to trust me. Let me help her. Please."

His words pulled me back just enough to meet his eyes, and what I saw there finally broke through the haze. Resolve. And something else. Fear.

My hands trembled as I released her, every fiber of my being screaming against it. Henry steadied me as the medics moved in.

I could only watch as they carried her onto the stretcher and immediately went to work on stabilizing her. Their actions blurred together, too fast and too slow all at once.

As they wheeled her away, I caught one last glimpse of her, so still, so pale. My chest tightened, panic spiraling into a suffocating weight.

"She'll make it," Henry said, his hand gripping my shoulder. "She's a fighter, Gideon. So are you."

But his words barely registered as my knees buckled beneath me. The ground rose up to meet me as my strength gave out, my hands bracing against the cold, blood-streaked concrete.

The last thing I saw before the darkness took me was the trail of blood Imogene left behind.

CHAPTER THIRTY-NINE

Gideon

The sunlight was blinding, even through my closed eyelids. I blinked against it, disoriented and uncertain of where I was. My feet were on sand, soft and warm but somehow not clinging to me. The air was thick with salt and the faintest hint of flowers, stirring something deep in my memory.

Hilton Head.

But as I opened my eyes, I saw it wasn't exactly Hilton Head. The colors were too bright, the edges of everything blurred as though I were looking through frosted glass. It felt like a memory come to life, beautiful, but not quite real.

And then I saw her.

Imogene.

She sat beside me, her legs tucked beneath her as the wind teased strands of hair across her face. Her eyes met mine, full of warmth and light, like none of the horrors we'd endured had ever touched her.

"Is this...?" My voice was hoarse, cracking like I hadn't used it in years.

Imogene smiled softly and placed her hand over mine. "Does it matter?"

I wanted to ask more, but she leaned in and pressed her lips to mine. The taste of her, the sweetness of her breath, the warmth of her touch drowned out every question.

For the first time in years, I felt at peace.

But our perfect moment was interrupted by a familiar bark. I looked up just as Ollie bounded across the sand toward a flock of seagulls, his tail wagging furiously.

"Ollie! Heel!" Imogene and I both shouted at the same time.

We shared a look before bursting into laughter. Ollie joined us, and I wrapped my arms around him as he smothered me with slobbery kisses, my chest aching with a mixture of joy and something else. Something heavier.

"This is it, isn't it?" I asked, looking at her. "We're dead."

Her smile faltered for just a second. "Do *you* think we are?"

I looked around the idyllic scene — the flawless blue sky, the gentle waves lapping at the shore. It felt like paradise. Our own personal heaven. But I couldn't shake the feeling that I didn't belong here.

"I don't know if I've earned this. I don't know if I deserve it."

Imogene squeezed my hand. "You're a good man, Samuel Tate." She leaned toward me, touching a kiss to my cheek. "But you're an amazing man, Gideon Saint. Never doubt that."

Our eyes locked for a brief moment before she stood up gracefully, brushing invisible grains of sand from her clothes.

"What are you doing?" I asked, squinting against the bright light behind her that cast a halo around her silhouette.

She shrugged. "I have to go."

Panic flared in my chest and I shot to my feet, reaching for her. But no matter what I did, she remained just out of my grasp.

"What do you mean? Where are you going?"

She glanced at Ollie, who stood at her side, his tail wagging slower now. "I don't know. It's just... It's our time."

"No," I pleaded. "You can't go. Stay with me. Please."

She faced me again, her expression tender but resolute. "It's time for you to go, too."

She started walking away, Ollie following obediently behind her.

"Imogene!" I tried to follow, but the sand beneath my feet seemed to hold me in place. "Come back!"

She didn't stop.

The world around me blurred, and her figure faded into the light. I screamed her name once more. This time, the sound wasn't muted. It was loud, causing me to startle.

Suddenly, everything was different.

The harsh fluorescent lights above me were blinding in a different way, the sterile smell of antiseptic replacing the salt and flowers. I blinked rapidly, my heart pounding in my chest as my surroundings slowly came into focus. The stiff sheets, the rhythmic beeping of monitors, the IV taped to my arm. Everything was sharper, more painful than the dream.

This was real. I was alive, stuck in some hospital bed.

But where was Imogene?

Did she somehow come to me in that dream to say goodbye?

The thought propelled me forward, and I forced myself to sit up. Ignoring the painful sting, I ripped the IV from my arm and swung my legs over the edge of the bed. My body trembling from the effort, I took a step, then another, pushing down the lightheadedness consuming me as I stalked toward the door that seemed to get farther and farther away.

When I finally opened it and emerged into the hallway, a brunette in green scrubs hurried toward me.

"Sir, you shouldn't be out of bed. You need to lie down and rest!"

"Where is she?" I demanded, my voice rough as I leaned against the doorframe for support.

"Please, you're in no condition—"

"Where is she?" I roared, shoving past her.

The hallway stretched before me, a maze of identical doors and glaring lights. I stumbled forward, my bare feet slapping against the cold floor.

"Imogene!" I bellowed, my cry echoing down the corridor.

I yanked open doors, one after another, each room that didn't contain the woman I was looking for feeding my growing desperation. My legs gave out briefly, sending me crashing into a cart of medical equipment, but I pushed myself upright again.

"Imogene!"

"Gideon."

The soft voice cut through the chaos in my mind.

I froze, unsure if it was real or I was simply hallucinating. Slowly, I turned toward the source.

She leaned in the doorway across the hall, her hair disheveled and her face pale.

"What are you doing out of bed, you stubborn ass?"

I crossed the hall in two unsteady strides, cupping her face in my hands. Her skin was warm and soft beneath my touch, her steady pulse a welcome relief.

Or perhaps an answered prayer.

"Is this heaven?" I asked, my voice trembling.

She let out a soft laugh, shaking her head. "I wouldn't call Los Angeles heaven, but it's not the worst place I've ever been."

The sound of her voice, the glint of humor in her eyes — it was real. *She* was real.

"What happened?" I asked, still struggling to process it all.

Her smile widened, a hint of mischief shining in her eyes. "Well, since you got a tattoo where mine is, I figured it was only fair I get a bullet wound where yours is."

She shifted her gown just enough to reveal the bandage covering her side.

I let out a shaky laugh, pressing my forehead to hers. Relief poured through me in waves, leaving me weak but lighter than I'd felt in years.

"I thought I lost you," I murmured.

"You're not getting rid of me that easily," she whispered back. "I took a bullet for you. You owe me now. And I intend on collecting."

I pulled her into a gentle hug, careful of her injury but unwilling to let go. "I'll gladly pay for the rest of my life." I tipped her chin back and touched a soft kiss to her lips, relishing in her warmth. Then I met her gaze. "And Liam?"

Her expression fell, and she gave a small shake of her head. "He didn't make it. One of the guards got to him just as Henry's team arrived. Slashed his throat."

I squeezed my eyes shut, letting this news sink in.

It was what I wanted for years, but it didn't feel as satisfying I imagined it would. I didn't relish in his demise like I thought I would.

"Now what?" I mused to myself.

Imogene pressed her hand to my cheek, forcing my gaze back to her. "Now we live happily ever after."

I inched my lips toward hers, the weight of the past five years evaporating. "I like the sound of that."

"As do I."

I still had dozens of questions. About how Henry figured out where we were. About how many more of Myers' victims were out there.

But I wasn't going to worry about that right now. Instead, I was going to do what I never thought I'd be able to do again.

I was going to live for the now. Not the past. Not the future. Just now.

Because that was all that truly mattered. This moment. This woman. And this love.

CHAPTER FORTY

Imogene

Atlanta had always been home, even when I hated it. It wasn't the city itself I'd wanted to escape. It was the memories.

But now, standing in the bedroom of the house Gideon and I had called home for the past few months so that I could be close to my parents, I saw the skyline differently.

The heavy weight I'd carried for so long wasn't there anymore. Maybe it was because Samuel Tate, *my* Samuel, was alive again — legally and in every way that mattered. The powers-that-be had restored his name and his life, and despite everything we'd endured, we were stronger for it.

Not that I'd started calling him Samuel or anything. To me, he would always be Gideon.

I checked my reflection in the mirror, hoping a sundress would be appropriate attire for whatever Gideon had planned today. The cruel bastard he was, he refused to give me any clues. All I knew was he wanted to spend the day making new memories together. To drown out the old memories this date held for both of us. After all, it was on this date six years ago I thought I lost him.

But he somehow found his way back to me.

And despite everything we endured, we managed to come out stronger.

Mere months ago, I didn't think I'd ever see Gideon again, let alone be able to start a life with him. I thought I'd die in that cell where Myers had imprisoned me, suffocating in darkness with only concrete walls and hopelessness for company.

And when all hell broke loose after I stabbed Myers, I thought I doomed us all. But I'd rather go down fighting than simply accept my fate.

Thankfully, Henry showed up like an avenging angel just when we needed him the most.

He had next to nothing to go on. Just the license plate of a van that turned out to be a dead end and what Gideon had told him during their last conversation —

that the man who took me confessed to being the man who also held him captive.

So Henry focused on that thread. It was thin, fragile, but thankfully it was enough.

He went back through the files Gideon had taken the night he killed McGuire. There wasn't much at first, just stacks of financials and coded transactions, but Henry dug deeper. He eventually traced a phone number McGuire frequently called to a pilot.

That in and of itself wasn't a giant red flag, but it made Henry suspicious, so he had some of his field agents track him down. After some forceful persuasion, he discovered the pilot often flew McGuire to one of three locations — Maine, Oklahoma, or Palmdale, California.

It may have been nothing, but Henry knew he had to do something, so he reached out to Melanie's father, Alexander, and they joined forces to storm a compound outside of Palmdale the pilot confessed to have driven him.

The FBI was horrified by what they found inside. Cages, recordings, and a vast network of atrocities orchestrated by Myers. Properties in Oklahoma and Maine tied to him revealed even more horrors.

As Gideon suspected, Myers *had* abducted Liam shortly after the recording of James Turner's conversation with Brian McGuire was leaked to the media. Then, to make sure it never came back to him, he requested to be assigned the case investigating Liam.

The entire investigation was essentially a game to Myers. An "experiment", as he called them.

And over the past several years, Myers had conducted hundreds of these experiments. The authorities said it would take years to unravel the full extent of Myers' twisted operations and identify all the victims.

All to feed his sadistic need to push people to their limits. To control them.

But he was gone and we could finally live the life we once dreamed about.

Now that we were back in Atlanta, Gideon's focus was on the community center he'd founded all those years ago, teaching at-risk kids how to channel their anger and aggression into martial arts. As for me, I ended my contract with the soccer team in San Diego earlier than I'd originally planned and start my own practice here in Atlanta. I still primary treated athletes, but I was now able to make my own schedule.

A sudden chiming cut through, the doorbell pulling me out of my thoughts. I checked the app on my phone, finding a man in a courier's uniform on our front porch with a small envelope in his hand.

I tried to bite down the grin begging to be set free as I rushed out of the bedroom and down the stairs, eagerly flinging the door wide.

"Imogene Prescott?"

"Yes," I responded breathlessly.

He handed me the envelope with a polite nod before disappearing down the walkway.

Unable to contain my enthusiasm, I tore it open and unfolded the single sheet inside. A familiar, masculine script greeted me.

> *You buried your nose in books galore,*
> *Lost in history, myth, and lore.*
> *But I preferred a hands-on class,*
> *Between the stacks, time seemed to pass.*

I didn't even have to think twice to figure out where to go — the library at my old college where Gideon would often drop by to visit me and give me a different kind of anatomy lesson than the one I was studying.

Hopping in my car, I made my way out of the peaceful neighborhood of Brookhaven and toward my old college, wondering if I should have taken an Uber to save time. But as luck would have it, someone pulled out of their parking spot just as I approached.

Once I killed the ignition, I grabbed my purse and hurried through the quad toward the library, finding the next clue in an anatomy book, as I expected.

From there, his clues led me across Atlanta. To a coffee shop. To a bench at Piedmont Park. Even to the building that was home to his community center. Each location filled me with a flood of fond memories and reminded me of the connection we shared.

Finally, when I found the last clue at The Varsity, where I rewarded myself with a Varsity dog, I knew I was nearing the end of my journey.

Past the trees and down the lane,
Where moonlit waters knew no pain.
The farmhouse waits where the lake is clear,
A chapter of our story I'll always hold dear.

Tossing out the rest of my half-eaten hot dog, I hurried back to my car, my excitement mounting with every mile. By the time I turned onto the gravel drive leading to my uncle's farmhouse, my chest was tight with emotion.

The house stood like a sentinel at the edge of the lake, its wide front porch bathed in the afternoon light. The sprawling oak trees that flanked it swayed gently in the breeze, their leaves whispering a melody only they could hear. The air carried the earthy scent of pine needles and fresh grass, mingled with the faint aroma of the lake water beyond.

Stepping out of my car, I paused to take it all in. The farmhouse looked the same as it did during my childhood with its whitewashed siding and green shutters. The creak of the wooden steps underfoot brought back memories of running up and down them with my cousins, and of one unforgettable summer night when Gideon kissed me for the very first time.

A fluttering erupted in my stomach as I climbed the stairs and opened the heavy wooden door, revealing the cozy interior I knew so well. Warm golden light streamed through the windows, catching tiny specks of dust swirling lazily in the air. The scent of aged wood and lavender cleaner filled my lungs, grounding me in the moment.

In the center of what once was the parlor stood Gideon, dressed in a sharp black suit with a single flower pinned to his lapel. My breath caught as I took in every detail — the way the suit hugged his broad shoulders, the way his eyes softened when they met mine.

"What's going on?" I asked, my voice barely above a whisper.

He stepped closer, his presence filling the room, the faint scent of his cologne teasing my senses. "I told you this morning," he said softly. "I wanted to give you a better memory of today. After everything we've been through, I think we both deserve that."

"You're right about that." I laughed under my breath.

"At first, I wasn't sure what to do," he continued. "I know you love scavenger hunts. But I wanted today to be special. A day you'll never forget. A day that will only conjure happy memories from this day forward."

I rose onto my toes and brushed my mouth against his. "Every day with you is the best day of my life."

His lips curved into a smile that made my knees weak. "Mine, too. And I don't want to wait another second to start the rest of my life with you, Imogene. I want it to start now. Today. Will you marry me?"

With a smirk, I held up my left hand, the engagement ring sparkling in the fading sunlight. "I already said yes. Or are you too old to remember that far back?"

He pulled me close and dipped his head toward my neck. "I should punish you for making fun of my age."

I met his eyes. "Promise?"

"You better believe it." His pupils dilated as he raked his gaze over my frame, causing heat to pool in my belly. Then his expression softened once more. "But that ring on your finger is just an engagement ring. I don't want to be engaged to you anymore." He brought his hands to my face. "I want to be *married* to you."

His statement hit me like a tidal wave, leaving me breathless. My pulse increased as I searched his eyes for any hint of hesitation, but there was none.

"Right now?" I asked, the words barely audible. "I don't have a dress."

"It's upstairs." He nodded toward the staircase. "Melanie and your mom picked it out."

Most women might have been upset at the thought of having someone else choose their wedding dress. Not me. I'd told my mom from the beginning that I didn't care what I wore. I only cared about who I was marrying.

"But my parents," I said, my voice faltering. "And Melanie. She'll kill me if I get married without her by my side."

His grin widened. "Your mom and Melanie are upstairs, as well. The rest of our guests will be arriving in two hours. I just need a bride."

Emotion swelled in my chest, threatening to undo me. A rush of joy, love, and disbelief coursed through me, leaving me breathless as I stared at the man who had defied every odd to find his way back to me.

The idea of getting married on a whim like this seemed so unconventional. But we'd never exactly been a conventional couple. Why start now?

"Okay," I whispered, the word catching on a sob. Tears streamed down my cheeks as I placed my hand in his. "Let's get married."

CHAPTER FORTY-ONE

Gideon

"Nervous?" Henry asked a few hours later, his voice low enough that no one else could hear.

He looked as composed as ever as he stood beside me in front of the makeshift altar, despite being forced to wear a suit.

"Not the way you're thinking," I admitted, shifting my weight.

My eyes swept over the people gathered to celebrate with us, their faces lit up by the soft glow from the lanterns swaying gently from the trees.

"It's more...anticipation. Excitement."

He smirked. "You're really doing it."

"I am," I said, glancing toward the farmhouse.

My pulse increased like it used to whenever I was about to be shoved into that cage to fight.

This time, it wasn't out of fear. This was out of pure joy. Although that seemed like too simple of a word to fully describe how it felt to finally be here. To finally marry Imogene.

It still felt surreal, like I might wake up back in the cell that had become my home for years. The outcome could have been so different if Henry didn't put the pieces together when he did. If he didn't follow his gut.

"I wouldn't be standing here if it weren't for you," I told him, meeting his eyes. "Imogene, either. I'll never be able to repay you for that, Henry."

"You don't have to repay me," he replied, his tone softer than usual. "But if we're keeping score, we're probably even after all the times you saved my ass back in the day."

"That was different."

"Not really." He clapped me on the shoulder. "You've always had my back, Sam. And now I get to stand here and watch you marry the woman of your dreams with nothing standing in your way."

"Thanks, Henry."

"I love you, brother," he said, though his voice cracked ever so slightly.

Before I could respond, the first notes of the processional music floated through the air. I flexed my hands, trying to channel the restless energy humming inside me.

The soft murmur of our guests and the rustling leaves faded into the background as I focused on the aisle that Imogene would soon walk down on her way to become my wife.

"Breathe, Gideon," Henry reminded me in a low voice. "I could be wrong, but most brides prefer their grooms to remain conscious for the ceremony."

I released a laugh, grateful for his grounding presence. But my attention snapped back to the farmhouse as the back door opened.

My heart leapt into my throat as Melanie appeared in a yellow dress, her dark hair cascading down her shoulders in loose waves. She carried a small bouquet of white roses, her smile radiating joy for her best friend.

She took her time as she made her way from the back porch and down the aisle. When she reached me, she threw her arms around me in a tight embrace.

"I'm so happy for you."

"Thanks, Mel."

She didn't immediately release me, as if wanting to stay in this moment that's been a decade in the making. When she finally let go, she dabbed at her cheeks before taking her place across the aisle from me.

Once she was in position, the music swelled, a subtle change in the melody that made my chest tighten.

I reminded myself to breathe, every muscle in my body taut as I waited. My vision tunneled, the farmhouse door the only thing I could see.

Then Imogene stepped onto the porch, her mother and stepfather on either side of her. Her dress was simple yet stunning, flowing around her in soft waves of ivory. Instead of a veil, delicate flowers were woven into her blonde curls.

For a moment, it felt like I couldn't breathe. Like my heart wasn't big enough to contain everything I was feeling. Like I had too much love inside of me.

There was a time I thought I'd never see her again. When every day was a battle just to survive. Back then, a future like this felt impossible. And yet, here she was, walking toward me, about to become my wife.

The seconds seemed to stretch as her parents slowly walked her down the aisle, all eyes focused on the stunning woman in white. I wanted to give her this moment, but at the same time, I wanted nothing more than to wrap her in my arms. Promise to love and cherish her for the rest of my life. Listen to our officiant declare us husband and wife.

"Gideon," her step-father said once they reached me, forcing my eyes from Imogene. He gave my shoulder a squeeze. "Take care of her."

I nodded, meeting his gaze. "Always," I promised before shifting my attention to her mother.

"We couldn't ask for a better man to love her."

"Thank you," I managed as I touched a chaste kiss to her cheek, my voice thick.

Imogene gave them both a kiss before facing me. I grabbed her hand in mine and steered her toward the altar, where her uncle Wes stood waiting with a kind smile.

"Ladies and gentlemen," he began, his voice rich with emotion, "we are here today to witness the union of two people whose love has withstood every test imaginable, Imogene Grace Prescott and Samuel Gideon Tate. Their story isn't just about love. It's about resilience, forgiveness, and the power of hope. And today, they're starting a new chapter together."

Imogene squeezed my hand, and I glanced down at her, meeting her sparkling eyes.

That was precisely where they stayed as Wes spoke about love and what a rare and special gift it was.

Finally, he looked my way and gave me the go ahead to share the vows I'd written.

"Imogene Grace Prescott," I began, losing myself in the depths of her eyes. "For years, I lived in the dark, believing there was no way out. No chance for anything good to survive inside me. But I didn't take into account one very important thing. From the moment I met you, you became my light.

"Even when I lost everything, the thought of you

kept me going. You are my hope, my heart, and my future. I promise to love you, to protect you, and to never let go of the joy we've found in each other. You've given me more than I ever deserved, and I vow to spend the rest of my life proving I'm worthy of it."

"You asshole," she choked out, which elicited polite laughter from our guests. "I promised myself I wasn't going to cry. And now I have to try to come up with something as good as that?"

"It's not a competition. Plus, I don't expect you to say anything, considering I sprang this wedding on you."

She swiped at her cheeks. "Oh ye of little faith. What do you think I did while Melanie worked on my hair?"

She closed her eyes and drew in a deep breath. When she returned her gaze to me, it was soft and filled with more love than I thought I deserved.

"Gideon." She treated me to a soft smile. "Samuel. You've always been my anchor. Even when life was at its hardest, even when I thought I'd lost you forever, you were still with me. You've shown me what it means to fight for love, to never give up, and to trust that some things are worth the risk. I don't know what tomorrow holds for us, but I know this. You are my past, my present, and my future. I plan on loving you every day for the rest of my life. Completely. Unequivocally." She smiled through her tears. "Unconditionally."

I smiled back, my heart so full it felt like it might burst. Then I repeated the only vow that would ever matter between us.

"Unconditionally."

In *The Count of Monte Cristo*, Alexandre Dumas wrote, "All human wisdom is contained in these two words — wait and hope."

I never put much stock into that famous last line. I never had to.

Now I understood them.

Hell, I *lived* them.

Hope kept me alive in my darkest of times. I didn't give up, even when I wanted to.

Now, I was able to live the life I always dreamed of.

With Imogene all my side.

All because I never lost hope.

CHAPTER FORTY-TWO

Henry

Rich people loved their masquerades, and this was no different. A fundraiser for clean energy, or clean oceans, or whatever the hell they were pretending to care about this week, while they snorted lines off marble counters in private jets. Hypocrisy had a stench, and it clung to this place like cheap perfume.

I hated everything about being here. The glittering chandeliers. The designer tuxedos. The conversations dripping with false smiles and ulterior motives.

But I was here for a reason, wearing a suit that felt more like a straitjacket and drinking scotch that cost more for a bottle than I once made in an entire year during my military days. I didn't belong here. I never did.

And yet tonight, I planned on playing the part of the billionaire philanthropist to perfection.

The crystal glass felt heavy in my hand as I leaned against the polished mahogany bar, the distant hum of laughter and polite conversation grating on my nerves. Every so often, I noticed a few people glance my way before whispering amongst themselves. They knew who I was. A recluse. Mysterious. Cold.

A genius billionaire who lost everything years ago.

And I was here to get it back.

The room was a showcase of wealth and pretense, a three ring circus.

And the ringmaster was none other than Victor Kane.

He stood in the center of the grand hall, his arm draped around his wife's slim shoulders, the image of a doting husband and magnanimous benefactor.

A fraud wrapped in designer labels and impeccable grooming.

I raised the glass to my lips, the smoky burn of the scotch doing little to dull the edge of my focus.

Years of combing through digital shadows, chasing whispers and breadcrumbs, and every lead had eventually brought me here.

To Victor.

The man with a sterling reputation and a soul dipped in sin.

His wife, Ariana, wasn't any better.

On the outside, she was poised and polished, her smile as practiced as his charm. But she was every bit as fake as the man beside her. They played their roles perfectly. The philanthropist and his adoring wife. Two sides of the same rotten coin.

The scotch swirled in my glass as I turned it slowly, my gaze never straying too far from Victor and his wife. But he never noticed me watching. Surveying.

Planning.

Why would he?

To him, I was just another billionaire who hoped to clear his conscience by donating to a good cause. My presence here was carefully orchestrated. An unassuming guest, blending into the background, letting the illusion of disinterest shroud my intent.

He'd built an empire of deceit, hiding his true self behind charity galas and glossy magazine profiles. But the cracks in his foundation were there, and I was going to rip them wide open. Piece by piece, I'd tear apart the house of cards he'd spent decades constructing. He just didn't know it yet.

Ariana's sequined dress caught the light as Victor placed a hand on her back, guiding her toward another group of sycophants. She moved with the grace of someone who thrived in the shadows of power, her every gesture calculated to support his image.

But she wasn't just a pawn. A piece of eye-candy. A woman without ambition.

She was his queen.

And if I learned anything from years of playing chess, the easiest path to a checkmate was by capturing the queen.

And that was precisely what I planned to do.

Thank you so much for reading *Final Vendetta*! I hope you enjoyed the final chapter of Gideon and Imogene's story!

Curious about what Henry's up to with Victor Kane? Find out in *The Hunter*. Just enter the link into your browser or scan the code below.

To take down a monster, you have to become one.

https://geni.us/HunterTK

Want one last taste of Gideon and Imogene? Then sign up for my mailing list to get a bonus chapter.

https://geni.us/Saint-Bonus-Direct

Wondering about everything Imogene went through as a teenager? Read Julia and Lachlan's story today and find out.

https://getbook.at/Temptation-Back

Thanks again for taking the time to read this book. If you enjoyed it, please let your friends know by leaving a review so more people can fall in love with Gideon and Imogene.

THE HUNTER

To take down a monster, you have to become one.

Years ago, Victor Kane destroyed my world. Now it's my turn to return the favor.

My plan? Burn Victor's empire to the ground... Starting with the perfect trophy wife at his side.

But the woman I expected to hate isn't what she appears to be. Behind Ariana Kane's icy perfection are secrets as dangerous as my own.

The deeper I fall, the closer I get to the truth...

And the closer I get to the one woman who could
ruin me.

To read Henry's story, scan below or type the address
into your web browser.

https://geni.us/HunterTK

ACKNOWELDGMENTS

Whenever I finish the final book in a series or trilogy, there's always a sort of bittersweet feeling. I started plotting this series right after I published *The Temptation Series*, since this is a spinoff of that. That was back in 2022. So I've been working on this story for the past several years. These characters have been a part of my life for the past several years. They've become like family to me.

While it's always bittersweet to finish a series, this one is even more so. While technically I've been plotting this trilogy out for the past two years, this has been the trilogy I've been wanting to write since I started publishing. I've always loved a good revenge trope, particularly like in *The Count of Monte Cristo*. I'm so happy I was finally able to write this story. And give Gideon the revenge he needed, as well as the redemption he deserved. I hope you enjoyed his journey, as well!

Before I start working on Henry's book, I wanted to take a minute to thank a few people who help make this all possible.

First and foremost, a huge thanks to my husband, Stan, and my daughter, Harper Leigh. I couldn't do this without their support.

To my wonderful PA, Melissa Crump — I can't tell you how much I appreciate everything you do for me.

To my fantastic beta readers — Melissa, Stacy, and Vicky — thanks for always reading and offering feedback.

To my admin team — Melissa and Vicky. Thanks for keeping my reader group and page running so I can spend my time writing instead of worrying about my social media.

To my review team — Thank you for always not only reading my books but also taking the time to write reviews. With the amount of books out there today, I'm grateful you're on my team.

To my reader group — Thanks for being my super-fans and giving me a place to go when I need a break from writing.

And last but not least, a big thank you to YOU — my amazing readers. I'm so grateful for your support.

I can't wait to share what's next.

Love & Peace,
~ T.K.

ABOUT THE AUTHOR

T.K. Leigh is a *USA Today* Bestselling author of romance ranging from fun and flirty to sexy and suspenseful.

Originally from New England, she now resides just outside of Raleigh with her husband, beautiful daughter, rescued special needs dog, and three cats. When she's not writing, she can be found training for her next marathon or chasing her daughter around the house.

facebook.com/tkleighauthor

instagram.com/tkleigh

tiktok.com/@tkleigh

bookbub.com/authors/t-k-leigh

pinterest.com/tkleighauthor